PAWSIBLY MURDERED

A Wonder Cats Mystery Book 9

HARPER LIN

NILES FREUDENFUR

"I can't believe we are doing this on our day off." I panted as I tried to keep up with my cousin Bea's pace. "Converse All-Star gym shoes are not really meant for exercise."

"Then what were they made for?" Bea asked.

"To look cool."

"You look really cool, Cath."

"I'd be sarcastic right back at you, but I have to catch my breath first."

"There's a bench. We can rest there." Bea slowed down to a stroll so I could stagger to the empty green bench at the side of the jogging trail.

"Am I really this out of shape? How fast is a woman my age supposed to run?" I gasped as I fell onto the bench, then I pulled my bottle of water from the fanny pack around my waist and took a deep drink.

"Run? I think it depends on how long you've been doing it. But you didn't run. You walked quickly... for a while... then you sort of slowed to a saunter, and that transformed into meandering."

"What about you?" I laughed as she tried to catch her breath. "When have you been secretly working out that you could keep trotting along?"

Bea shrugged.

Since we were children, Bea and I had been opposites. It was part of what made us grow up as the best of friends. Bea could walk into a room, and people would instinctively be drawn to her. It was part of her empathic gift.

Since childhood, Bea could not only see auras but also heal people. Everyone just thought it was her more-than-loving disposition that left them feeling better after being around her. But there was so much more to it than that. It was one of the most dramatic differences between us.

I could speak telepathically with animals and, in most instances, preferred their company to that of humans. I especially enjoyed the company of my cat, Treacle. He had a very sarcastic streak in him. Birds of a feather, they say.

But back to my cousin. When I would look at a grumpy person, I'd see a grumpy person. Bea, on the other hand, would look at a grumpy person and see they had a blockage or tear or lesion on their essence. If they were receptive to her, as they almost always were because she was so pretty, with naturally bright-red hair and kind eyes, they'd allow her to touch them, holding a hand or stroking an arm, even patting their shoulders. The relief from their malaise would be almost instantaneous.

To them, Bea was just one of those people who made you feel good when you were around her. However, it wasn't always so easy. In order to heal, Bea had to give a little bit of herself to the person in need. That would sometimes take its toll on her. She might suffer a bad headache or have to lie down for an hour or two. Other times, it would be like the day after a night of drinking, only without all the alcohol.

Due to the fact Bea's gift could be so taxing at times, she insisted on eating healthily and was strictly vegan—something I could never do.

"You know what this regimen needs? Bacon." My eyes widened, and I began to salivate at the thought. "And not that turkey bacon or tofu bacon. I mean real off-the-pig bacon."

"I've got breakfast waiting for us at home." Bea

smiled. She looked as if she were ready for a sporting-wear photo shoot in a cute pair of turquoise running leggings and a T-shirt splattered with turquoise, black, and gray colors.

I didn't even want to think of what I looked like. My ponytail was falling down, and half of it was stuck to the sweat on my face. When Bea had suggested we exercise in the park, I grabbed a pair of baggy gray sweatpants that I usually reserved for those uncomfortable days of the month when I wasn't quite myself or if I was suffering due to the cold and flu season. Up until today, the idea of exercising in these sweatpants had never crossed my mind. I also had an oversized T-shirt that doubled as pajamas when the weather got warmer. But at least I was wearing my most stylish red Chuck Taylor Converse All-Star gym shoes.

"You've got breakfast ready? Great. Mind if we jog to Burger King over on Fifth Street on the way home?"

"If I thought you could make it, I'd say yes."

We both laughed. I was happy when Bea took a seat next to me. There was no way I could get up and run any farther. My legs were trembling, and my lungs were happy that I'd slowed things down. Okay, I didn't slow them. We stopped, and I was glad.

"It really is a beautiful morning," Bea said, taking a deep breath.

"Yeah. Have you and Jake got your patio furniture outside yet?" Jake was Bea's husband and the brother I never had.

"We do."

"Can we sit outside and have breakfast? Please? Please? Please?"

"I knew you were going to say that. Of course we can."

"Yay." I loved sitting on Bea's back porch. It was flanked on each end by two huge oak trees that kept it in the shade continually. Bea had hung crystals and wind chimes from the branches. No bird feeders, though. Her cat, Peanut Butter, was still in the wild and crazy stage of a young cat. Scaling the trees in an attempt to capture a robin or a cardinal was a small feat, especially if it resulted in a kill to present to Bea.

"So, what is for breakfast?"

"It's a surprise."

"Bea, just tell me if there is tofu in it. I'll know how I'll have to proceed from there. Is there tofu?"

"No. Not a single cube of tofu. Not that a little bean curd wouldn't be good for you. But no. No tofu."

I was about to make another sarcastic remark when I saw a woman jogging toward us, waving and smiling.

"Is that Lawanda Riggs?" I pointed.

Bea turned and looked. "It is." She smiled and waved back.

Lawanda came to the Brew-Ha-Ha Café often. She was also wearing a matching running outfit, putting me to shame.

"I thought that was you guys. The Greenstone women on the workout path." She puffed. "Is this going to be a regular routine for you two?"

I said no at the same time Bea said yes.

"Well, at least you have a plan," Lawanda joked. "Hey, are you guys going to that huge estate sale?"

"Where is it?" I asked. I loved estate sales. Not because I was necessarily looking to buy anyone's stuff. I was more interested in seeing the insides of the houses.

"Niles Freudenfur's house."

"What?" Bea and I said, again speaking in unison.

"You guys didn't hear?" Lawanda put her hand to her mouth.

Both of us shook our heads no.

"They found him dead in the house. He'd been there a couple of weeks." She wrinkled her nose.

"What happened?" Bea asked.

"He was old," I said. "Probably just had a grabber."

"You have to use the term grabber, don't you?" Bea shook her head. "You can't just say 'had a heart attack.' You have to say grabber."

"Well, that's what happens," I said matter-of-factly. "They grab at their hearts when they have the attack. I'm not being rude. I'm just being literal."

Bea rolled her eyes.

"Whatever you want to call it, they are opening up the house today around eleven," Lawanda said. "I always wanted to see what that place looked like on the inside. If it's anything like Niles, it ought to be interesting, to say the least."

"Right. The guy wore a cape to get coffee," I said.

"He only did that once, and he said he was going to a concert at the Wonder Falls Symphony Center," Bea defended.

"Sure. I saw him wearing it at the grocery store," I said.

"You're making that up."

"What would be the point of making up a story about creepy Niles Freudenfur?" I looked at Lawanda. "Did you ever meet him?"

"I saw him at the bank every Thursday, and he was wearing a cape."

I looked at Bea and tilted my head to the right, raising my eyebrows.

"I'll say this too." Lawanda stepped closer and lowered her voice. "That guy was making big deposits in his bank account for the last few years. He'd come up to my window a couple times a month with two thousand, sometimes three thousand dollars cash. That was in addition to the checks from his antique business. I'd never ask him where he got it. But I wondered."

"He had that side business of reading tea leaves and casting bones. People will pay a lot of money to be told what they *want* to hear." I smirked. In my eyes, no one but my Aunt Astrid, Bea's mom, gave honest, real tarot, bone, and tea readings.

Aunt Astrid could not just see the future, but she could also see the past, the present, and a couple alternative dimensions thrown in for fun. It caused her to walk as if she had been in an accident that limited her mobility. Truthfully, she was just maneuvering around some of the things only she could see. No one would ever suspect she was a witch with great power. For that matter, no one would guess Bea and I were witches, either. And we liked it that way.

"So, are you guys going to go to the sale?" Lawanda asked.

"I am." I raised my hand. "You bet. That house makes the Norman Bates *Psycho* house look like a day spa."

"You are crazy," Bea said. "That is a lovely home. Niles was in his seventies. He couldn't very well keep up with all that property. What did he own? Somewhere around ten acres of wooded land all alone up there on that hill? That might have been manageable when he was in his thirties, but it probably just became too much for him."

"It isn't like he lived on an island." I scoffed. "He had neighbors across the street. I'll bet we'll meet all of them when we go to the estate sale."

"And they'll tell you he was a harmless old man who was a little on the eccentric side but nothing more," Bea insisted.

"Yes. Aside from the times he stripped nude and ran around his yard, howling at the full moon," I joked.

"Wearing his cape," Lawanda added, making her and me laugh loudly.

Bea shook her head and clicked her tongue at us.

"Okay, I'll stop," I said. "I'm just joking around. I

didn't like Niles, but I never heard he ran around howling at the moon. I just made that up."

"Well, I have to get going if I'm going to get any benefit out of running this morning," Lawanda said. "If I don't see you at the estate sale, I'll catch you around the café."

We said good-bye to Lawanda as she jogged down the path that we were supposed to go down to complete one lap around the park.

"I don't feel much like running anymore. Do you?" Bea asked.

"Nope. But I would like to hurry and tell your mom the news about Niles."

"You were reading my mind."

We didn't run, but the little bit of town gossip refilled our tanks so that Bea and I were able to walk briskly back home.

"I'll meet you on your porch in ten minutes," I said as I ran to my house. It was kitty-corner to Bea's, and just two doors down from Bea's house on the same side of the street was Aunt Astrid's home.

"Okay. We'll eat fast and go to Mom's."

I waved and ran to my front door faster than I had all morning at the park.

2

WITCHES IN DAYLIGHT

I showered in record time at my house and threw on a pair of blue jeans with a white T-shirt. It was shaping up to be a beautiful sunny day that was not too hot or cool. I trotted over to Bea's and let myself in, ready to discuss what we'd just learned on that very educational jog.

Bea had made a really lovely breakfast of chocolate oatmeal with fresh fruit and honey along with iced mint tea. But both of us scarfed it down so fast while talking about Niles that we barely tasted any of it. Surprisingly, by the time we headed over to Aunt Astrid's house, I felt as though I'd eaten three eggs, two sides of bacon, and some toast with jelly.

"That breakfast was good," I said.

She linked her free arm through mine, pulling me

along to her mom's house. Peanut Butter was snuggled in her other arm, content and used to the trip down the block. We didn't bother to knock on the front door. Instead, we walked around to the back and slipped through the new privacy fence my aunt had put in.

Contrary to popular belief, witches adored the daylight, sunshine, birds chirping, and bumblebees buzzing. We liked to pay homage to the beauty of daylight and those things that moved about in it. So in order to perform some of her daytime rituals, Aunt Astrid thought a tall fence would ensure her safety and privacy.

Plus, it provided a little extra safety for Marshmallow, Aunt Astrid's cat. She was the oldest among our familiars. Like Aunt Astrid, Marshmallow moved slowly and deliberately. After living at least half of her nine lives, Marshmallow had more knowledge and experience than Treacle and Peanut Butter combined.

Aunt Astrid was adding dirt into a large terra cotta pot. There were bright-pink petunias in a tray next to her. Unlike Bea's old-fashioned-looking porch, Aunt Astrid had a rather simple patio of red brick. At the end of it was a small fire pit. The yard was not filled with lush, thick vines growing in all directions with eye-popping blooms on all of them. Like me, Aunt Astrid didn't have a very green thumb.

But the few pots she had placed around had flowers growing in them, and the neatly trimmed grass was pleasant to walk in if you liked the feeling of grass on your feet. I never did. But Bea did and immediately kicked off her shoes.

"How did the exercise go?" Aunt Astrid asked without looking up.

"Wait until you hear," Bea said as she set Peanut Butter down and wiggled her toes while standing next to her mother. I took a seat on one of my aunt's extra-cushy patio chairs. It had cushions so thick that when you sat down, you didn't feel the bumps and ridges of the wicker. Peanut Butter took off after a butterfly.

"Niles Freudenfur is dead."

"Niles Freudenfur is dead?" Aunt Astrid gasped and stopped what she was doing to gape at me. "That doesn't sound right."

"It's true. We ran into Lawanda in the park. She said there is an estate sale at his house," Bea added.

"Did she say what happened to him?"

"Grabber," I piped up, winking at Bea.

"He was in the house for two weeks before they

found him." She wrinkled her nose as Lawanda had done.

"I'm totally shocked." Aunt Astrid sat back on her haunches, her eyes wide. "Niles was in his seventies, right? I don't know how to feel about this." My aunt looked as if she were trying to remember the answer to a question—the same look I had while taking just about every test in any subject in high school. "He and I weren't friends. In fact, I told him to stay far away from me. He claimed to be a psychic, but his methods of contacting the other side were questionable at best. Dangerous at most. I didn't want him anywhere near you girls or me."

"Cath and I are going to go to the estate sale at his house. Do you want to come?" Bea asked.

"Yeah, come on, Aunt Astrid," I said. "Maybe you'll see something you can use."

"We'd have to do a thorough psychic cleaning of everything we take out of that house. Not to mention a good old-fashioned scrub down with soap and water. I'm sure his entire house smells of clove cigarettes."

"I like that smell," I admitted.

My aunt and Bea looked at me funny, so I quickly changed the subject.

"Did Jake know anything about this?"

"Good question," Bea said. "I'll give him call."

She strolled past her mom and me into the house. Bea had a cell phone that she kept at her home, so she was using Aunt Astrid's landline. Bea was convinced that the waves from the phone not only affected your brain but also deteriorated the natural strength of your life force. I agreed with her.

Meanwhile, my aunt continued to knead and spread the dirt from the bag with a big yellow sunflower on it to the pot.

"That stuff kind of stinks," I said.

"It's got nutrients and things in it to help the flowers grow."

"Like poop?"

"Cath, the universe has a use for everything natural in the world. Even poop."

"Doesn't mean we should put our hands in it." I tried as hard as I could not to smile or giggle when my aunt looked up at me. But it was no use. I giggled like a twelve-year-old boy who saw butt steaks were on sale at the supermarket.

Just then, a familiar black cat slunk over the fence.

"Hey there, handsome," I said in my mind.

"Hi," Treacle said, strutting over to me, and gave my calves an affectionate rub with his furry body.

Within a few minutes, Marshmallow appeared and slunk out of the sliding screen door that Bea had left open.

"Marshmallow, where have you been?"

"Waiting," she meowed.

"Waiting for what?"

"For this." She strolled over to a perfect square of sunlight that was coming through Aunt Astrid's vinery lattice and fell over.

Treacle, who found a similar square just a couple inches away, did the same thing.

"It seems like it took a long time for spring to finally get here. We've been cooped up inside forever," Marshmallow said.

She yawned while reaching out a playful paw to touch Treacle. He responded with a whip of his tail.

"Staying close to home today? That's a little unusual. Are you feeling okay?" I asked my black cat as he purred loudly.

"I feel fine. I'm just in the mood to be lazy. Besides, I left you a present already this morning. It's on the kitchen counter."

"You are so thoughtful," I gushed, knowing that there was going to be a dead bird or a dead snake or a dead baby rabbit on my counter when I got home.

I stooped over and scratched them both behind the ears just as Bea returned.

"Well, Jake heard about it. But he said he didn't have a grabber." Bea looked at me.

"What happened to him?"

"Jake said he and Blake were called to the house after a uniformed officer was making a welfare check."

According to Bea, a neighbor had noticed mail and newspapers piling up outside.

"When they got there, the uniformed officer was all choked up. Niles had some strange stab wounds, but they weren't life-threatening and might have been self-inflicted. But the officer thought Niles had choked on something he was eating."

"I never thought of that," I said.

"But…"

"There's a but?" I sat up straight.

"There were weird marks around his neck and some strange slimy stuff on his clothes." Bea's right eyebrow shot up.

"Foul play?"

"Jake says they haven't said yes and they haven't said no. It's still being looked into."

Marshmallow and Treacle were sleepily watching us when Peanut Butter decided to turn her attention to them. I watched the smaller orange cat stealthily creep closer and closer. She nestled quietly in the grass, her eyes wide with mischief, her back end wiggling as she revved her engine, then *boing*! She sprang in a perfectly silent arch and came down on Treacle, who leaped straight up in the air. When his feet hit the ground, he took off after Peanut Butter. They rolled around over and over each other in the grass as I laughed.

"What are you two up to?" Aunt Astrid yelled playfully. They froze and snapped their heads in our direction. I laughed even harder.

"They are just playing. Peanut Butter snuck up on Treacle. She's getting to be quite the predator." I looked at Bea, who beamed with pride.

"I know what happened." Aunt Astrid pushed herself up from her flowerpot and pulled off her gardening gloves. "He probably tried to do some spell, and the whole thing backfired on him. Accidental suicide."

"That's awful," Bea said. "To be snuffed out like that due to your own unsteady hand."

"It *is* awful," my aunt continued. "But there was no telling Niles Freudenfur that he was doing it wrong. He came from a long line of Third-Eye Seers, he'd say. Whatever that meant. In all my books, I never found the name Freudenfur. Of course, his answer was that the name morphed and changed over the centuries. He had an answer for everything."

"You know what else is awful? That home of his was beautiful," Bea said. "I heard around town he had quite a collection of expensive antiques and furniture and books and paintings."

"Where did you hear that?" Aunt Astrid asked.

"Just around town. Sometimes people would ask if we were affiliated with his psychic readings."

"To which you responded with a resounding *no*." My aunt was on a roll.

"Of course." Bea nodded. "But you know how some people are. If you charge a fair price and have a simple setting for people to visit you, you are the hack. Not the guy who charges a small fortune and has you visit his elaborate home that screams of old Vincent Price movies."

"That really is awful." My aunt shook her head.

"What's really awful is that everyone is going to get to the estate sale before us and get all the good junk," I said. "Can we make like a tree and leave?"

3

SANCTUM TOTEM ARCANA

The Freudenfur estate was a painted-lady-style house and the only one of its kind on Barbour Street at the edge of town. It was yellow with white trim and black shutters. There were three stone steps that led to the front door. The old mail and newspapers were still piled up there. The remnants of police *Do Not Cross* tape were stuck around the open door.

I looked in the bay window, which was wide open, and could see people milling around. Of course, I also looked at the second floor and at the oval attic window, expecting to see Niles's gruesomely distorted face peering out. All that was there was a pretty lace curtain.

Two people were coming out of the house, but

they had nothing in their hands. They also seemed to be hurrying away. But that was normal. They might have gotten a phone call to be somewhere or maybe had only stopped in to peek.

"There's Lawanda," Bea said as she put her car in Park.

"I'm surprised we caught her," I said as I unbuckled my seat belt on the passenger's side. "In fact, at the rate you were driving, I'm surprised we caught the sale at all."

"Hey, better safe than sorry." Bea stuck her tongue out at me.

We all piled out of the car like clowns and approached the front door.

"Lawanda!" I waved.

She smiled awkwardly and came up to us while rubbing her arms as if she were cold.

"What's the matter? Didn't find anything good in there?" I asked.

"I don't think I've ever seen such beautiful things. But well, I don't know." Lawanda scratched her head. "Maybe it's because he died and was in there for a while before anyone found him. I just didn't want to buy anything. Truthfully, I didn't want to touch anything. I know it's just because I watched too many scary movies growing up." She chuckled nervously. "I don't know. Maybe you guys will have better luck."

Lawanda waved good-bye and hurried to her car.

I looked at Bea then realized Aunt Astrid was already going up the steps.

"For someone who didn't like the guy, she sure is in a hurry to look inside," Bea joked.

"She's not the only one," I said.

When we stepped over the threshold, I was shocked that Aunt Astrid had been so spot-on. The place did smell like clove cigarettes. But there was something else, like a mossy smell.

"My mom is over by the books." Bea jerked her chin. "I'm going to go and check what's upstairs."

The next thing I knew, I was by myself, so slowly, I began to roam from room to room but was stopped quickly by a cheery voice to my right.

"Welcome. If you have a question about any of the items, just let me know." It was one of the sales coordinators. She was wearing enough makeup to audition for a Las Vegas show, and her hair was poufy around her face.

"Thanks. I'll bet you are selling a lot of stuff. This guy was known to be quite a collector," I said, just to be polite.

"You'd think," she whispered. "We've had a lot of

foot traffic, but practically no one is buying anything."

"Really?"

"I've never seen anything like it. People are saying the prices are good. They love this lamp or that set of silverware. But when it comes time to buy it, they say they feel funny and change their mind."

I wanted to dash up the stairs and see what Bea was feeling throughout the place, but that would have been rude.

"We just had a few people purchase some new sheets that were still in the packaging and a bookcase that was from Ikea and still in the box. Meanwhile, that beautifully etched corner bookcase is waiting to be taken to a good home for only twenty dollars."

"Twenty dollars for that dark-wood bookcase?"

I pointed, and the woman nodded.

"What is your name?"

"Dorothy McGill. But you can call me Dot." She handed me a business card.

"Well, Dot, wrap it up, because I'll take that bookcase."

Dot smiled happily. I told her I was there with my aunt and cousin and would like to look around a little more. When I made it to my aunt, I told her everything that Dot had said.

"If you could see what I see, you'd understand why people aren't buying." She shook her head.

"What is it?" I asked.

"Everything has got cobwebs on it. Psychic cobwebs. Layers upon layers. Like Niles never did a smudging to cleanse the house. I find that odd because he had the most meticulous fingernails every time I dealt with him."

"Weird."

"It is. Unless he was more of a fraud than I thought." She looked back down at the books. "Aside from all these New Age-y books, I'm surprised Niles didn't have something with a little more meat, even if it were just for show."

"I'm going to keep looking around."

I got a nod from my aunt, who went back to sifting through the stacks of books.

Dot had done an excellent job of displaying everything that was for sale. As I had expected, Niles had tons of candles, paintings in gilded frames, crystals of all sizes and colors, sound bowls, and thick, heavy furniture. The cushions were bright red, and the frames were a rich dark brown and chiseled into clunky blocks. It was the tackiest furniture I'd ever seen and came in a set of eight, including a couch, a love seat, two armchairs, a coffee table, an end table, and two lamps. His guests had to go crazy seeing that furniture in candlelight just before some make-believe séance or tarot reading. I had to admit the presentation was impressive.

That was another thing I noticed. There were stacks of tarot cards that looked as if they were homemade. I was all for an arts and crafts project, but whoever drew the pictures on these cards, I hoped they didn't quit their day job. They were horrible designs and garish colors. It was obvious that some of the creatures were supposed to be angelic or fairylike. They looked more like starving fashion models and, instead of walking on a runway, were floating in water or dangling from a tree. So it was hard to tell which cards represented what. Others had pointy teeth and wild eyes.

No one was looking to purchase these. I didn't blame them.

The paintings propped up along the walls were of similar designs. I squinted and saw that N. Freudenfur was scribbled in the corners of all the pieces.

"Not only could he see the future, but he was an artist too. A jack of all trades."

The funny thing about this was that everything in the house looked as I expected, but precious little of it was authentic. I stood in the middle of the room and imagined what it would look like with nothing but candlelight and violin music playing in the background. I'd swear I was in a villa in Transylvania. But turn the lights on, and it was like a real painted lady when the sun came up.

As I roamed around, I peeked out the windows into the backyard. There was a lot of vegetation and what looked like a pond or some kind of round altar out there. I was going to go sneak a peek, but the door wasn't just locked. There was a second deadbolt, a chain, and a two-by-four across it.

"There has got to be something of value in this house for Niles to have this many locks on the back door," I mused.

I thoroughly inspected the main floor, and still there was nothing but the bookcase to strike my fancy. There were lots of people milling around, and I was happy to see someone buy a silver salt-and-pepper-shaker set. They were probably spray-painted that color, but who was I to ruin what that person liked?

I went upstairs to see if Bea had stumbled upon

anything. I wasn't sure what to think when I saw her expression.

"Are you okay?"

"Yes," she said with tight lips.

"What are you pinching your lips for?" I asked while pinching my lips.

"I don't know what to think about the room down the hall."

"Why?"

"I can't explain it. You have to see for yourself."

I squinted at my cousin, wondering if this was a trick. When she didn't move or start to laugh, I walked down the dark, wooden hall to the last room. The door was open. Inside were shelves and shelves of dolls.

Some of them were obviously old. Their clothes were faded, and some of the paint on their faces was chipped, giving them a sinister appearance, to say the least. Others were newer with frilly dresses and oodles of curls on their heads. Each one of them stared straight ahead. Or maybe they were looking at me. I wasn't sure. I didn't want to find out.

If anything in the house gave me the creeps, it was that room filled with the dolls. I was never a doll person.

"Freaky, right?" Bea asked when I walked back to her.

"I'm not sure what to think of that. Niles Freudenfur was a doll collector?"

"Maybe. If I were to guess who in the town was a doll collector, he would probably be on the short list. The cape. The flamboyant personality."

"Yeah," I said. "But he was such a know-it-all about other stuff. I wonder what prompted the pursuit of dolls."

"I guess we'll never know," Bea said in a spooky, whispery voice.

"Let's check out the bedroom."

I was not the least bit surprised by what I saw in there. Niles had a four-poster bed with curtains draped at the head. Satiny sheets and comforters were folded neatly with little price tags on them. The matching dresser and night-stand were of the same dark wood. There was a beautiful mirror, but it had a crack up the center.

"I have to admit, I was expecting so much more. This is not a cheap piece of property, but Niles does not have the taste I thought he did," I said.

"Did not."

"What?"

"*Did* not have the taste you thought he did. Past tense. He's dead now."

"What about you? Are you getting any sense of something inside this place? I feel like I'm walking through the Museum of Natural History, looking at those cheap-looking replicas of the day in the life of a Neanderthal man or the Mayans."

"There is definitely something wrong with all of this. But I can't lock in on anything. I was hoping to go up in the attic, but it's locked off. I'll try the kitchen since it's the heart of the house."

Before we left the bedroom, a bright flash caught my eye.

"What is that?" I pointed toward the closet. It was wide open, but there was another little door inside. The light through the window caught on the crystal doorknob, grabbing my attention.

"I don't know about that." Bea slipped her hand in mine. "Those kinds of doors are always creepy."

"I agree. But let's peek anyway."

While holding hands as though we were no older than twelve, Bea and I walked into the closet together. I reached down and turned the doorknob. It click-clicked then gave way as the latch was pulled back. Gently, I pushed it in.

"It's pitch black in there." I peeked. "Go in there

and look around."

"I'm not going in there." Bea shook her head.

"Are you getting any vibes?"

"Nothing," Bea said.

"Fine. It's probably just an empty storage room. These estate people look through every nook and cranny of a house. I'm sure everything that is out is all there is."

"Let's find Mom."

I shut the little door as Bea walked out of the closet first. That was when I heard a loud scream. Not a human scream but some kind of thick-throated animal that was outside. Bea was already out of the room. I hurried and looked out the window. The glass was filthy. I couldn't tell what I was looking at. From where I was, I didn't see anything. I held my breath and listened, but all I heard was the people bustling around downstairs. Now I was wondering if the sound was outside or inside. As if I heard something inside my head.

"Residual effects, Cath," I said to soothe myself. "That was probably the sound Niles made when he was dying. Maybe."

I shook it off and went after Bea. When I found her with her mom, they were both looking like the cats that swallowed the canaries.

"What are you up to?" I whispered.

"You won't believe this," my aunt said, hushed. She looked around to make sure no one was too close to her. "Niles has the first edition of *Sanctum Totem Arcana*. This book is so valuable in the realm of witchcraft that there have been generations of witches that had dedicated their lives to finding and protecting it. Even killing for it."

"Do you think that someone might have done Niles in to get the book?" I asked.

"No. I don't think Niles even knew what he had. Look." She pointed to the faded green color of the hard cloth cover. "There are rings of dried wine on it. I found a recipe for meatloaf stuffed behind one of the pages. I think he kept this out on the coffee table for effect."

"Tell her the best part," Bea bubbled.

"They've got it priced at five dollars." My aunt's eyes danced with giddiness.

"Wow," I whispered. "That's a real find. Maybe we should hurry up and get out of here."

"I think you are right."

Aunt Astrid shuffled to where Dot was still sitting. With lightning-fast reflexes, she gave the woman a five-dollar bill and hustled outside. I paid for my bookshelf and was happy it fit in Bea's trunk.

Once we got home, Aunt Astrid, Bea, and I did a quick cleansing spell over our purchases in her backyard. Happy to have gotten rid of any of Niles Freudenfur's bugaboos, I lugged the bookshelf across the street to my house and propped it in the kitchen. I saw Treacle's gift on the counter. A lovely gray mouse with pitch-black bug eyes.

"Thank you." I shuddered.

I decided to lock the front door for the rest of the night. If anyone needed me, they'd see me bright and early at the café in the morning.

I put on my favorite classic movie station and almost squealed with delight when I realized *On the Waterfront* was on. I quickly took a shower, made myself a bologna sandwich with potato chips and a pickle, and ate it before tackling the bookcase.

As usual, I got sucked into the movie, then the next one was *Guys and Dolls*. Not a great Marlon Brando movie, but there was no denying how handsome he was. I sat through it and cleaned the bookcase during the singing parts.

I stopped mid-song when I realized there was something strange about this bookcase. The bottom shelf had a fake bottom. And there was something in it.

❧ 4 ❧

FAKE BOTTOM

"Hey! Wait for me!" I shouted out my front door as Bea started walking to work. I struggled with my sweater, slammed the door shut, and nearly tripped over Treacle, who had snuck out the door before I could close it.

"Be a good boy, and be home before dark."

"I'll try," Treacle replied as he slunk around the side of the house and out of sight.

"You aren't going to believe what I found." I panted as I raced up to her. Normally, we didn't walk together to work. Aunt Astrid owned the Brew-Ha-Ha Café, so she was almost always there first. Bea was up early, making breakfast for Jake and some-times his partner, Blake Samburg, so she usually moseyed in second.

I liked to wait until the last possible moment to get up. So I almost always brought up the rear. But this time, I was up as early as Bea.

"What?" she asked, yawning.

"That bookshelf from Niles's estate sale had a fake bottom."

"What do you mean?"

"There was a secret compartment in it."

"Please don't tell me there was a doll in there." Bea's eyes were wide.

"No. But I have the feeling it might be equally creepy." I reached in my bag and pulled out a leather-bound book. "It was wrapped in a towel and stuffed in there with this strange statue that's at the bottom of my bag."

"Is this his diary?"

"I just glanced inside, and then I shut it. It is his diary."

"What does it say?"

"I didn't read it." I took a deep breath and let it out slowly.

"Cath, I'm so proud of you," Bea said, as if she were describing a UFO to the police over the phone. "But that is a little out of character for you. You're a bit, well, you know."

"Nosy?"

"I didn't want to be mean." Bea grinned.

"Believe me when I tell you that I think it was the hardest thing I ever did."

"You didn't read it."

"Nope." I folded my lips over my teeth.

"Not a page," Bea pushed.

"Not really." I was feeling my resolve start to wane.

"How much of it did you read?" Bea handed it back to me.

"I just read a couple sentences. It freaked me out." I felt my cheeks blushing.

"Oh my gosh, Cath. You are turning all kinds of shades of red. What on earth did you read?"

"Can we just wait until we get to the café? I don't want to have to repeat myself."

"Is it that bad?"

I shrugged.

Bea took my hand, and we finished the last two blocks to the café at a healthy jog. I was winded and very concerned about whether my deodorant was going to hold up when I finally handed the book over to Aunt Astrid. After I told her where I'd found it and that I'd only peeked at it, Aunt Astrid took the book, opened to a random page, and began to read.

"Well, this doesn't surprise me." Aunt Astrid closed the book.

"Can someone tell me what all the hubbub is?" Bea asked as she made the coffee in the giant silver urn.

"It seems that Niles had a young love interest. A good bit younger."

"How young?" Bea asked.

"From the sound of it, he was still excited about showing his ID to buy wine at the liquor store," I said, shrugging.

"That young? Yikes. A May-December romance." Bea whistled.

"That's not a May-December romance. That's more like a BC-AD romance."

I chuckled at my own comparison. When no one else laughed, I cleared my throat.

"So, which one of us is going to read it and tell the others all the gory details?"

"We can't read it," Bea said. "That's someone's diary."

"Normally, I'd agree with you. But that someone is dead. So I don't see it being any kind of scandal anymore. Go ahead, Aunt Astrid. Crack that sucker open and start reading." I rubbed my hands together.

"I am going to read it but not out loud." She gave

me a look as though I'd suggested we all wear bikinis to work the next day. "This might help us figure out a few things."

"Yeah, like why Niles had a room full of dolls." I looked at Bea.

"Maybe. But I'm thinking it might be helpful in figuring out how he died."

"Yes. That would be a good thing to figure out too." I snapped my fingers. "Good thinking, Aunt Astrid."

I didn't know what I was expecting, but when Aunt Astrid put the book in her purse and took a seat at her favorite table next to the counter to work on a grocery list for the café, I slouched with disappointment.

"I should have read the whole thing when I had the chance," I said to Bea.

"No. You did the right thing, Cath," Bea assured me. "Mom will tell us everything."

"I know. I just really like gossip." I couldn't help but laugh and bump Bea with my hip.

As luck would have it, business at the café was very slow. It started as a cool sunny morning and turned into a cloudy day threatening storms.

So I didn't say anything when I saw Aunt Astrid

retrieve the diary and start reading. It didn't take long until she read something that troubled her.

"What is it, Mom?" Bea asked.

"I'm starting to feel a great deal differently about Niles," she admitted.

"Why? What was wrong with him? Aside from the dolls," I asked.

"According to this, he was pursuing this young man. The one you opened up the page and read about. He details how he followed him, learned his routine, showed up at places where he knew he'd be. It's crazy."

I looked at Bea but didn't say a word. This was a little more than I'd expected.

"In between, he's writing about a couple of clients who are regulars. He's speaking horribly of them."

"Is he a fraud like you thought, Mom?"

"No. Not completely. He did have some psychic ability." My aunt looked troubled. "But like with anything, too much can make you lose your perspective. I think..."

"What?" I was leaning against the counter, waiting for my aunt to finish her thought.

"Listen to this: *I can feel the presence whenever someone comes for a reading now. It's like an old friend showing up. The trade-off might be a little odd, but it has worked all this time. I can't wait to share it with Patrick."*

"What in the world does that mean?" I scratched my head.

"I don't know." Aunt Astrid stared at the book. "But that is one of the last entries that makes any sense. A few pages along, you get this: *Dirty. Filthy. It was filthy. A disgusting thing that wanted to touch me. But I hid. I hid in that place and liked the dark. It will avenge me. I know it will."*

"That sounds like dementia," Bea said sadly.

"Maybe. But I'm still convinced that he did a spell wrong and lost his marbles," Aunt Astrid said. "There could be nothing more than shadows in his house, but he saw monsters because he used rosemary instead of sage or lit a red candle instead of an orange one. Unfortunately, our history has plenty of examples of this. Careless witchcraftery."

"What does he want avenged?" I asked.

Bea and my aunt shrugged, yet my aunt continued to speak.

"Probably the fact the squirrels were digging in his yard. Like I said, I think he made himself crazy with a spell gone wrong. I'll bet if we track down this Patrick guy, we might find out something."

That was going to be difficult since nowhere in

Niles's journal did he mention a last name. However, he did give a rather detailed description of the guy. Rather than canvass the neighborhood with sketches of what we thought Patrick might look like, I had a better idea.

"Was there an appointment book?" I looked at Bea. "If Niles was doing readings up to the end, he had to have their appointments written down somewhere. Maybe Jake would know if they had that in the evidence or something."

"But if it's in the evidence room, we can't get to it." Bea slumped.

"We don't need the book. We just need Patrick's last name. Jake might already have the guy on his people-of-interest list," I said.

"I'll ask him tonight when he gets home."

5

PERSONA

The next morning, Bea was the last one to arrive at the café.

"What happened to you?" I asked while stroking Treacle, who had slunk in through the open back door shortly after we opened.

Kevin Baker, our fabulous and intensely introverted chef, almost always left the back door open so the hot air from the ovens would escape and cool air would come in. Treacle, who roamed the neighborhood daily, would find his way back here when there was nothing more exciting happening in the world. Or if it was raining.

"I was up all night with Jake."

"Too much information." I held up my hands. "Bea, we don't need to know."

"Climb out of the gutter for a minute if you can," she squawked. "This has to do with Niles Freudenfur."

"What did you find out?" Aunt Astrid asked.

Before Bea could say anything, a familiar face entered the café.

"Good morning, ladies." Tom Warner looked dashing in his police uniform. He walked up to me. "Miss Greenstone. You are looking lovely this morning. Give us a kiss."

"Are you drunk?" I asked.

Tom and I had been dating for several months.

"No. I'm on duty." He leaned forward, offering me his cheek, tapping it with his index finger.

I couldn't resist. His cologne smelled spicy, and his cheek was smooth after shaving. I gave him a quick peck before Bea and my aunt could say anything.

"Good morning, Treacle," he said, scratching the spoiled cat behind his ears where he especially liked it.

"Hello, Tom. Pull up a chair and stay awhile," Treacle purred loudly.

"You've had enough attention, kitty," I replied.

I only got a lazy wink in return.

"So what are you doing here so early?" I asked Tom.

"I've got a visitor coming to see me, and I'd like you to meet her."

"Her?"

I'm not a jealous person. Okay, well, I can be but not like a Glenn Close, *Fatal Attraction* kind of jealous. But when a guy wanted to introduce his girlfriend to a woman, it had better be his mother.

"Why, Miss Greenstone, are you jealous?"

"No. I've just been waiting for you to show your weird side, and I'm guessing this is it." I folded my arms across my chest. "Who is she?"

"My mom."

"Oh." I gushed and smiled like an idiot. "I didn't know."

"She just got back from travelling through Europe."

"Wow." I gasped. "How long was she gone?"

"Almost a year. She was spending a little time in each of her favorite countries. She has some friends over there. Anyway, this is her first stop back in the States, then she is going to visit my sister and brother."

I tried to calculate in my head how much it would

cost to spend a year in Europe, but math was never my strong suit. I settled on it being a lot of money.

"I'd love to meet her," I said.

"She's going to love to meet you too," he said, stepping closer to me again. "Here. I picked you up a little something the other day. I thought you might like it."

He handed me a box the size of a credit card. I opened it up and started to laugh. It was a little silver witch on a chain. She had green crystal eyes and was riding a broom.

"This is so adorable." I quickly showed Bea and my aunt.

"Tom, that is really sweet." Aunt Astrid chuckled. "I'll take one, also, but I prefer gold."

"Mine should be in rose gold to go with my hair," Bea added.

"I'll see what I can do," Tom replied, smiling. "Are you free tomorrow evening? We can go for a late dinner."

"She's free," Aunt Astrid answered.

"Totally free," Bea added.

"That sounds fine." I was smiling so much my cheeks were hurting.

"We'll pick you up here around seven." He kissed

me again on the cheek and hurried out of the café after kissing Aunt Astrid and Bea on the cheeks as well.

"Meeting the mom? This is getting serious." Aunt Astrid stood from her table. "What do you think, Bea?"

"When Jake asked me to meet his mom, I knew he felt the same way about me that I felt about him. But meeting mothers can be tricky." She blinked.

"How many mothers have you met, Bea?" I teased.

"It's not tricky," Aunt Astrid said soothingly. "Just be yourself. Sometimes the mothers are more nervous meeting you than you know. This is so exciting. Bea, what do you say we get this place looking extra special nice for our future in-laws."

"Aunt Astrid, aren't you jumping the gun a little bit? I don't know if I want to get married. Besides, no one has even said the "M" word until now, and it was me, so it doesn't count."

"We aren't worried about you. It's about making *us* look good," Bea interrupted. "Mom, what do you say we break out those Fourth of July decorations? It's never too early in the summer for red, white, and blue."

"You are going to decorate this whole place just for this one woman?"

"No. Our patrons will like it. Won't you?" Bea asked a fellow sitting by himself in the corner with the newspaper in front of him.

He nodded.

"See?" Bea bustled to the back of the café, where all our holiday decorations were kept. Within minutes, she was back, dropping one large box on an empty table. Before I could say anything else, she disappeared then reappeared with another box.

"That should do, Bea," Aunt Astrid said as she walked over to the table. They opened the box and began rifling through the patriotic knickknacks while I stood back.

It was sweet of them to go through all this for me. I looked down at the charm Tom had given me. As I took it out of the box and fastened it around my neck, I couldn't help but think something wasn't right. This wasn't how I expected things to unfold.

"Oh, I love this guy!" Bea squealed and held up a rustic-looking overweight Uncle Sam.

It was cute. I smiled. But I couldn't shake what I was feeling.

"*Are you okay?*" Treacle asked.

"I don't know," I replied. *"Maybe I'm just surprised. I wasn't expecting to meet the parent today. Especially when Niles Freudenfur is still dead and it may or may not be a murder. Am I selfish for wishing this were happening any other day than this one?"*

"I don't think so. I just hope she likes cats."

"Deal-breaker if she doesn't."

I stroked my cat's shiny black fur for a second then went to help Bea hang some metallic streamers from the ceiling. They looked like fireworks.

"So what did Jake tell you about Niles?" I asked, happy to get the attention off me.

"I almost forgot." Bea shook her head. "As it turns out, Niles died almost two weeks ago. The police department had been keeping it under wraps as they tried to search for a next of kin. Turns out Niles had a sister."

Aunt Astrid gasped. "Was she from around here?"

"Nope. Lives all the way in Maryland. Said that she and Niles had a falling out because of his lifestyle."

"His preferring-younger-men lifestyle?" I asked.

"No." Bea looked down at me from the stepstool she was balancing on. "Because of his occult lifestyle. She said he had this idea of being the next Aleister Crowley."

"Of all the people to model your life after, he picks that con man?" I snickered.

"That explains quite a bit." Aunt Astrid was placing the fat Uncle Sam statue next to the register. "Crowley created the persona so there was no way for anyone to argue he was doing the whole satanic thing wrong. Niles really followed that formula, except…"

"Except what?" Bea carefully came down from the stool so I could climb up.

"Except he wasn't interested in a 'religion.' Niles was all about the money."

"How do you know that?" I asked.

"From what you said Lawanda told you about his deposits at the bank."

"That isn't all." Bea put her hands on her hips. "The police went through the house long before the estate-sale people did. They collected several books written by Niles, and according to Jake…"

"What?" My eyes were wide.

"He said they scared him. He wouldn't tell me what was in them."

"Maybe he'll tell me. Get him on the phone. I'll

ask," I said. "Tell him I'm not afraid to rough up a cop."

"Calm yourself, Cath." Aunt Astrid patted my shoulder. "Will he tell me?"

"I don't know. But he said that since the books and other pieces of evidence came into the station, he's noticed something weird happening."

"Weird like lights blinking on and off or weird like people levitating and spinning their heads all the way around?" I asked.

"Weird like this brown substance keeps showing up in the evidence room around the books and other things they collected," Bea said. "I stayed up last night putting a protection spell on Jake. I'm confident it will hold. Peanut Butter was a great help. But Blake is out there. You know how skeptical he can be."

"We can't worry about that right now," Aunt Astrid said. "Blake is a grown man, and he doesn't take unnecessary risks. So far, nothing is hurting anyone. So I think what we need to do is go back to Niles's house."

"What will that do?" I frowned.

"Maybe nothing. But maybe I can get a past impression of some of the things that had been going on in that house that might point us in the right direction."

"When are we executing this caper?" I looked at Bea, who was yawning. "That one won't be any good to us in the state she's in. I'm going to have to have a talk with Jake and tell him to quit keeping you up all night. You aren't honeymooners anymore."

"Very funny." Bea yawned again.

6

PINK AURA

Since the foot traffic was so slow, Aunt Astrid and I sent Bea home to get some rest. As the afternoon changed from bright blue to a subdued purple, one of Aunt Astrid's regular customers came in for a tarot reading. Her name was Beverly Connors. She was a very pleasant woman who Bea said had the calmest, most tranquil pink aura she'd ever seen. I didn't know exactly what that meant, but according to Bea, it was a good thing.

"Hi, Bev," I said as she came in carrying her giant leather purse that she always had with her. It was stuffed to maximum capacity—with what, I couldn't say. If anyone were to ever push her in a body of water, I knew that purse would sink her to the bottom faster than rocks in her pockets. "Aunt Astrid is in the back."

I jerked my thumb toward the back of the café, where my aunt had her table and tarot cards set up. I heard the two women greet each other and have a little friendly chitchat before a hush fell over them. Aunt Astrid barely spoke above a whisper when she gave her readings. Privacy was as important to her clients as it was to her.

I served a couple of teas and coffees, and much to my utter disappointment, I served Kevin's last double-chocolate cupcake that I had been going to take home with me if no one bought it. There were still three lemon poppy cupcakes with lemon frosting on them. It wasn't my first choice, but they had frosting. I'd be taking them home instead.

"Hi, Cath. Let me have those three lemon cupcakes to go," Beverly said when she emerged from the back.

"Of course." I smiled as I said farewell to the tasty little morsels.

"Your aunt is just the sweetest thing," she said. "Do you know that I don't think she's ever been wrong about my future since I started coming to her. She's just a wonderful gift."

"Oh, I'll be sure to tell her you said so." I handed

Beverly her change and the box of cupcakes. "I can't help but agree with you one hundred percent."

"Have a good night." She hoisted her purse over her shoulder and left the café in a tinkling of chimes.

The last two coffee drinkers left as well, and I flipped over the Open sign and locked the front door behind them.

"A little good luck came our way with Beverly Connors," my aunt said when she emerged from the back.

"Oh yeah? Tell me," I said as I started to move the tables to start the sweeping.

Since she was a fan of tarot readings, Beverly admitted to Aunt Astrid that she had, once upon a time, gone to Niles Freudenfur. She said that he insisted all the readings be done in his house, and there was a rather large sitting fee.

"How large?" my aunt had asked her.

"Well, he gave me a discount the first time, so it cost under fifty. But anything after that and anything that went over a certain period of time would run almost two hundred dollars," Beverly said with a frown. "But I wanted to give him the benefit of the doubt. You get what you pay for, right? Sometimes you have to spend money to save money."

"I understand," my aunt admitted. The last thing

my aunt wanted was for Beverly to feel uncomfortable.

"So I get to his house, and I see where all the money goes. He's got enough incense floating around you can barely breathe. There were lots of candles and some New Age music in the background. But it didn't go with the spooky atmosphere. It was like a mishmash of corny stereotypes. He also had another person sit in with us."

"Really?" Aunt Astrid was shocked.

"This young man, dressed very neatly with short red hair sat in on my reading. Now, I'm no prude, but this is my first experience with this reader. I'm not sure what he's going to see. How do I know this young man isn't part of some scam?"

"Do you happen to know the man's name?" Aunt Astrid asked, crossing her fingers under the table.

"Patrick. Patrick Fouts. I remember because Niles spoke more to Patrick than he did to me. I think there was a little something going on between them. Normally, I wouldn't care. However, this was on my dime, and a lot of time was being wasted while these two played footsie under the table."

Beverly scooted in her seat.

"They didn't really play footsie, but you know what I mean. As I was saying, by the time Niles finished telling me his credentials, a move that I think was more to impress this young man than me, I had had it."

"What did you do?"

"I told him that I needed him to get on with it or that I'd have to reschedule, and I wasn't paying for this visit of just sitting here."

"And what did he do?"

My aunt was shocked by Niles's strange behavior. She had known him to be eccentric. We all knew that. But this sounded more narcissistic than anything else.

"He finally shuffled the tarot cards and gave me a reading that took about five minutes." Beverly folded her hands in front of her. "This may sound crazy, but his reading was spot on. The problem was all the stuff I mentioned. I didn't want a stranger in the room, listening. I certainly didn't need all the visual effects. And well, Astrid, I enjoy coming here. I trust you. Your daughter and your niece are beautiful girls and so friendly. I could probably do without the cupcakes, but they are so delicious." Beverly laughed. "If it ain't broke, don't fix it."

"Do you know of anyone else who saw Niles on a regular basis?" Aunt Astrid asked.

"Unfortunately, my neighbor Dolores Eversol."

Beverly leaned in. "She's a bit of a handful, if you ask me."

"Why do you say that?"

"Very high-maintenance. Her husband is a lawyer and out of town a lot. She has a blank check for anything and everything she wants to do. Straight from the horse, I know she doesn't make any decisions without consulting Niles first." Beverly had rolled her eyes. "The poor thing probably doesn't know if she should wipe her nose or her aaa... pardon me. I'm getting too worked up."

"So we struck gold with Beverly Connors stopping by," I said, rubbing my hands together. "Patrick Fouts and Dolores Eversol. Which one do you want?"

"Hold your horses. We need to have a meeting of the Greenstones before we go diving into all this." My aunt knew I didn't like waiting.

"Oh, yeah, sure, of course." I nodded.

"Cath. I mean it."

"What? When have I ever made you worry?"

"Do you want a list?"

IT WASN'T THAT I INTENTIONALLY WANTED

to upset my aunt. But to me, there was no time like the present. I looked in the phone book, and as clear as day, there was one listing for Eversol. That wasn't exactly a common name, and the address was just a hop, a skip, and a jump from the Mariano's grocery store. I liked that grocery store, and as luck would have it I was out of milk. I had been out of milk for almost two weeks, but I decided that tonight, at nine o'clock, I needed to go get some milk.

Before I hopped in my car, a familiar dark shadow came skulking around the side of the house.

"*Where are you going?*" Treacle asked. He sat at the front door, waiting for me to open it back up for him. He could easily get in through the kitchen window that was cracked for him to get in and out, but like me, he was nosy.

"*I've got a lead on a possible suspect.*"

"*You're going alone?*"

"*Why? Would you like to come with me?*"

"*Sure.*" He licked his paw then looked up at me.

As if he had all the time in the world, Treacle slunk toward the car and hopped in. Within a few minutes, he was current on what I'd learned from Beverly.

"*Do you think it's a good idea to go to this stranger's home at this hour?*"

"*It's not that late,*" I said. But Treacle had a point. I didn't know how receptive I'd be to someone knocking on my door at that hour to ask about a friend who just died.

"*I've got an idea. She'll be none the wiser.*"

"*I'm intrigued. Do tell.*"

❧ 7 ❧

KINDRED SPIRITS

"Treacle! Treacle!" I shouted as loud as I could underneath Dolores Eversol's porch. "Treacle! Here kitty, kitty!"

Just as we planned, within a few minutes of shouting and stomping around, Dolores came to the door.

"Can I help you?" She looked down her nose at me from behind her locked screen door.

"I'm so sorry," I blubbered. "My cat, Treacle, ran under your porch. He got chased by someone's dog on the next block. But I know he's under there. Treacle."

A soft meow came from behind the steps.

"Did you hear him?" I said, pretending to cry a

little. "He's just scared. He'll come to me. Here kitty, kitty. Good kitty."

I got down on my knees and peeked under the steps. Treacle was right there, but we had a good act going.

"I'm so sorry, ma'am. Could I bother you for a saucer of milk? That'll get him out quickly. I know it will."

Dolores looked quite put out, but she nodded. Within a few minutes, she was back at the door with a saucer.

"You know, my psychic told me something like this was going to happen." I chuckled. "I thought I was going to lose my purse. Turns out I held tight to my purse and let loose of my cat."

"You consult with a psychic?" Dolores's hard shell started to crack as she opened the screen door and handed me the saucer.

"Well, I did until he died. Thank you. This should do the trick."

"Oh, don't tell me that you consulted with Niles Freudenfur."

"That's him. I only received the benefit of his guidance twice, but he really made an impact," I lied.

"I was a patron of his for over five years. He was a brilliant man." Now it was Dolores's turn to start crying. "I was more than a patron to him, I must say. We were kindred spirits."

I set the milk down and took a seat on the step so as not to spook Mrs. Eversol. She was the perfect example of what a good plastic surgeon could do. Her hands and throat were wrinkled, putting her around fifty years old. But her face was smoother than mine, and her eyes, although clear and bright, had obviously been tugged to the side, making them narrower than normal. Her lips had been plumped up as well as her breasts. She wore yoga pants and a T-shirt with a sweater. The air-conditioning was set for freezing in her house.

"I don't know what happened to him," I lied again. "I went to schedule a visit, and there was an estate sale going on. No one said anything except that the owner of the house had died. Did you hear anything?"

"Well, speaking as someone who knew Niles very, very well, I suspect that he was murdered."

"Really?"

"He wasn't the only psychic in town. But he was the best. When you are as good at your craft as he was, there are bound to be some haters." She folded her arms and tugged at her sweater. "Like the witch down at that café."

My mouth fell open.

"I don't go to that part of town, usually. But there is a café that is run by some woman, and she does tarot readings. I wouldn't be surprised if she had something to do with this. I mean, you have to wonder about a person who only charges twenty dollars for her gift of sight. Or should I say her gift of story-telling."

I swallowed hard and tried to think of something to say.

"Niles told me how jealous she was of his business." She looked at me with that air of self-importance.

I went to speak, but the words stumbled and tripped all over each other until I finally got control of my tongue. "That sounds a little too far-fetched to me." I cleared my throat. "Maybe Patrick had something to do with it. The man who sat in on his sessions."

"Absolutely not. Patrick adored Niles. In fact, Niles confided in me that they were lovers."

"He told you that during a session you were paying for?" I wanted to push Dolores just a little.

"Well, as I said. We were kindred spirits. There was a mutual give and take." She nodded. "I was like a sister to him. He even told me that since he had no family, he was grateful to me for accepting him."

"That is really nice." I pretended to look under the porch. "I think he's getting closer." Treacle let out another meow for effect.

"He had told me that he thought I was gifted. I just needed the proper training and guidance to reveal it."

I didn't ask any further questions. It was obvious that Dolores was very interested in talking. No need to prod or interrupt.

"He said that my soul had experienced several life cycles and that in each one of them I was in a position of power. Sometimes I was a male. Sometimes a female. Sometimes an animal."

"An animal?" I said. "That's deep."

"Isn't it? That's why I can communicate with them."

"Really?" I was getting angrier by the minute. First she insulted Aunt Astrid, and now this. "Do you think you can communicate with Treacle and get him to come out?"

"Oh, well, I can only communicate with dogs. I was a she-wolf."

"Darn." I snapped my fingers and frowned.

"Ha ha ha," Treacle laughed when I peeked under the steps.

"Here, kitty. Some nice milk for you."

"I just don't know what I'll do without him. Niles was such a big part of my life."

"Sure." I watched as Treacle drank the saucer of milk.

"At least I'm getting something out of this," he said as he lapped slowly.

"I am too. A headache."

"He told me he was on the verge of completing a progression of rituals that would allow him even greater visions. He thought I'd be a good candidate to follow him, you know, as a pupil."

"Do you know what the names of these rituals are?" I didn't expect her to know. It was obvious I was dealing with someone who enjoyed being the center of attention. Even if it meant diminishing the fact that a man's life had come to an end, Dolores was the one really affected.

"The Sequence of Ursaken."

My breath caught in my throat.

"Did you say *The Sequence of Ursaken?*" I looked at Dolores as if she'd just sprouted tentacles and a second head.

"Yes. It's supposed to take several weeks to

complete and must be followed to the letter. Niles was going to have me prepare and perform it with him, but I've got responsibilities here at home."

I grabbed the empty saucer and handed it to Dolores.

"Treacle." With one leap, the big furry lump was in my arms. "We have to go now."

I didn't say thanks or good-bye. There wasn't time for those kinds of formalities. The truth was I was a swirling ball of fear, anger, and astonishment.

"That was rude of you," Treacle said as I carried him down the block to where I'd parked my car.

"Are you kidding me? What's rude is that woman making Niles's death all about her. Past lives and talking to animals. If she was an example of the kind of people who paid money to Niles for his psychic guidance…well, I don't even know what to say about that. And what about her talking about Aunt Astrid the way she did?"

"That was out of line," Treacle concurred.

"I was ready to slap her across the face. It makes me wonder what else Niles said about her. What kind of a psychic talks about other people to his clients? He's supposed to be telling them about their lives, not his own."

"What is The Sequence of Ursaken?" Treacle asked as we reached the car.

Within seconds, I had my Dodge Neon turned

around, speeding home. I knew I was going to get in trouble for visiting Dolores on my own. But it was worth it.

"The Sequence of Ursaken *is a long, drawn-out ritual that is nearly impossible to perform. Aunt Astrid will have all the details. All I know is that it is something to stay away from.*"

I hit the gas to catch a yellow light and quickly made my way down the quiet subdivision street to my house. You could imagine how shocked I was to get honked at by Bea just as she was pulling into her driveway. Aunt Astrid was in the seat next to her.

Bea spoke before I could.

"Do you want to tell us what you learned from Dolores Eversol? We struck out finding Patrick Fouts."

"Why, you sneaky witches." I smirked.

8

THE SEQUENCE OF URSAKEN

"I can't believe that woman would accuse Mom of having something to do with Niles's death," Bea spat. "What a piece of work."

"I can't believe Cath didn't punch her in the face." Aunt Astrid laughed.

"Treacle was so good in his role, I didn't want to blow our cover." I sat in Bea's kitchen, sipping a chamomile tea. "But it was very hard. The more Dolores spoke, the harder it was to listen. This whole crime isn't about Niles. It's about Dolores Eversol and how she is going to cope."

"That was a great idea to get to her," Aunt Astrid concurred. "Well played, Treacle."

He barely opened his eyes from the armchair by

the sliding back door. Peanut Butter was snuggled up tightly next to him.

"But what about *The Sequence of Ursaken*? I remember you telling Bea and me when we were teenagers to stay away from that. To not even read the list of ingredients, let alone try to perform it."

"I remember that too," Bea said.

"It backs up my theory that Niles is the victim of his own hubris." Aunt Astrid helped herself to one of Bea's sugarless sugar cookies. "But I have the feeling that Patrick may offer us a little more help. If we can ever find him."

"Are those cookies any good?" I asked, unable to help myself.

"Of course they are good. I just use applesauce instead of sugar," Bea said.

"So they are applesauce cookies?"

"No, they are sugar cookies, but I used applesauce."

"So they are fraud cookies."

"Don't you ever get tired of being a nerd?"

"Do you?" I popped the cookie into my mouth. It tasted delicious.

"All right, girls. This is serious. If Niles Freudenfur decided he was ready to perform *The Sequence of Ursaken*, there is no telling what damage he might have done." My aunt looked serious as she looked at her watch.

"How tired are you girls?"

"I've got a little more juice left in my battery."

I looked at Bea and shrugged.

"I'd like to go back to Niles's house." Aunt Astrid's face was grave. "I obviously missed something when we were at the estate sale. I know why too."

"Why, Mom?"

"I was too wrapped up in my own suspicions about Niles. I let it fog my vision. I wanted proof he was a fraud even though I already knew he was one. I knew with his money that he probably had some items I could never hope to have. Aside from the copy of *Sanctum Totem Arcana*, I didn't see anything of any value. But I was looking through a lens of envy. I guess I was suffering from a severe case of hubris too."

My aunt's face was drawn down.

"You know what? We need to stop what we are doing," she said. "This time, I'm serious." She looked at Bea and me intently. "I've got to cleanse my own house, so to speak, before I can proceed any further. If Niles was dabbling in things that were over his head, I should have helped him understand them."

"Did he ever act like he wanted your help?" I asked.

"No. But that doesn't mean you don't offer it. It doesn't mean you hope in your heart for the person to fail so you can feel legitimized. That's what I was doing. I was feeling superior to Niles, knowing full well that he had no idea what he was doing. Smoke and mirrors. That was all he offered. I was the real deal." She sighed as she slid off the seat at Bea's kitchen island. "I'm going home, girls. I'll see you tomorrow at the café."

Without another word, Aunt Astrid left.

"I've never seen her that way," Bea said. She wrung her hands.

"No."

"I don't think my mom ever acted conceited or full of herself. Why is she saying this stuff?"

"Let's be honest. Only she knows what's going on inside her."

"But I should know too. What's the use of having empathic senses if they can be so easily ignored when I don't like someone? I didn't feel anything at that house. Or maybe I didn't want to." Bea scratched her head.

"What do you mean?"

"I looked around that house too. I stumbled across that room full of dolls, and I made a judgment that Niles was even weirder than we all thought he was."

"Let me stop you right there. A man in his seventies with that many little-girl dolls *is* weirder than we thought he was. You can't sugarcoat it. Mix in a little applesauce so the disturbing facts go down a little easier." I shivered.

"But..."

"But nothing. I only saw what I saw. Maybe the next time we go, we should bring the familiars. If Aunt Astrid's vision is clouded and your senses are muddied, then maybe the cats will see clearer than all of us."

"That's a good idea."

"Of course it is. But I will say this." I took another cookie. "If we have reached a point where I'm the only one making sense, then we all might be in big trouble."

With everything going on, I had nearly forgotten about meeting Tom's mother. Did it mean something that I wasn't as excited about this as some girls would be? Once Treacle and I were home for the night, I was getting nervous over the fact that I wasn't all that nervous.

"Not all girls have the kind of family you do."

Treacle was eavesdropping on my thoughts. I must have been thinking extra loudly.

"You think that's it?"

"I don't know."

"A lot of help you are." I scratched him between his ears.

As I was lying in bed, my mind was focused on how weird Dolores Eversol was. I tried to concentrate on what I was going to wear to meet Tom's mother and what I'd talk about. But my heart just wasn't in it. I kept drifting back to Dolores. She spoke about Niles as though he walked on water. I had to wonder if she knew about his room full of dolls. Would that have changed her opinion of him?

"She's not a killer. I can see her being one of those women who catch mice in humane traps and let them loose in fields and forests nearby. Of course, she'd have to brag about how she did it."

Treacle looked up at me from the foot of the bed but said nothing.

Sleep finally came at about two thirty in the morning.

9

MUD

W hen I finally dragged myself into the café, I could see by Bea and Aunt Astrid's faces that I looked like a kid who hadn't studied for midterms.

"I couldn't sleep," I confessed.

"Worried about tonight?" Bea asked.

"What's tonight?" I asked as I poured myself a cup of strong black coffee.

"You're meeting Tom's mother," Aunt Astrid said.

"Yeah. I guess so." I let out a deep breath. "I just couldn't sleep last night. With all the stuff we talked about last night, it's hard to focus on something so simple."

"Meeting his mother is simple?" Bea gasped. "I

wish I had your confidence when I met Jake's mother. Speak of the devil."

Just then, two shadows crossed the storefront window. When the chimes jingled, I turned around to see Jake and his partner, Blake, walking in.

"Hey, honey." Jake leaned over the counter and kissed Bea on the cheek.

"Detective Samberg."

Aunt Astrid always fawned all over Blake. He had no family and was a bit of an oddball. My aunt loved that about him.

"How are you this morning, honey? We haven't seen you in a while."

"Hello, Aunt Astrid. The chief has been keeping us busy." He turned to me. "Hello, Cath."

I yawned and waved.

"Late night on the town?"

"No. Insomnia," I confessed before slurping some of my coffee.

"I wish I'd known. I suffered a bout of it last night as well." He looked back at my aunt. "Niles Freudenfur's case is getting more and more bizarre with every person we talk to. Not to mention I've got a stack of files on my desk six inches high of cases I haven't even been able to glance at, let alone make any progress on. I'm fortunate insomnia and the occasional heartburn are my only afflictions."

"Have you made any progress?" Bea asked Jake as she held his hands over the counter.

"You guys look so sweet I'm getting a cavity," I said.

"Funny." Bea rolled her eyes. "Just wait until it's you and Tom."

"Oh, yeah, tonight you are meeting his mother." Jake grinned. "Are you nervous?"

"You're meeting whose mother?" Blake asked.

"Tom's," I answered. "No. I'm not nervous. Tom is a normal fellow. I'm sure his mother will be normal too."

"That's them. What about you? I'm not sure the term *normal* applies." Jake was enjoying himself a little too much.

"Not with you in the family, Jake," I snapped back before another yawn got me.

"*Sui generis,*" Blake piped up.

"Bless you," I replied.

"No. I didn't sneeze. I was referring to you. *Sui generis.* That means alone or singular. I categorize you as *sui generis.* If I *had* to put you in a category." He pouted his lips as if he were really pondering the thought. "Wouldn't you agree, Astrid?"

"I would, indeed."

My aunt didn't bother to hide her expression of approval toward Blake. I was not sure what she saw in the guy, but sometimes I wished she were forty years younger so she could date him herself.

"Well, no one is categorizing me just yet. What's in the folder, Jake?" I was happy to change the subject. Plus, Jake had a folder under his arm that had pictures in it. I could see them peeking out enough to recognize the telltale crime-scene-photo coloring. "Can I see?"

"I don't think you want to. It's Niles after he marinated in his house for two weeks."

"Okay. Maybe your wife and my aunt are squares, but I'd like to take a look." I looked at my aunt and then at Bea.

"Jake, if you don't mind, I'd like to take a look too," my aunt said.

Blake took a seat at the counter next to his partner and took the file from him. I set a coffee cup in front of Blake and filled it for him.

"You take it black don't you, Blake?" I asked.

"Yes," he muttered without looking up. That was typical and one of his habits that drove me absolutely crazy. Not a thank you. Not a gracias. Not even a smile. There was no limit to Blake Samberg's snooty behavior.

Among the pictures was the coroner's report along with diagrams of the male form. Any wounds were marked in red pen on the body. The reason for death was listed as asphyxiation.

"He was choked?" I said in a hushed voice. Three of the tables in the café were occupied. One was a college-aged girl who had her head down and earbuds in. I wasn't concerned with her overhearing us. But there was an older man reading the paper and two middle-aged women who were chatting quietly. They didn't need to hear about Niles's condition.

"More like *he choked*," Blake replied and showed me a photocopy of the crime scene. Niles's eyes were wide open. His mouth was frozen in a grimace of terror more than pain, and his hands were curled into jagged claws at his own throat.

"What is all that?" Bea pointed to his neck. "Is that...blood?"

"No. It's primarily mud. There is some algae and slime mixed in with it. But it's mostly mud," Jake said.

I looked at my aunt. Her expression was not what I'd expected. Whenever we were faced with a strange or unfamiliar or out-of-place thing, something in my aunt's face usually indicated she knew what we were dealing with. She might not have an exact name, but she'd have an idea of what we might be up against. I found courage and comfort in that expression. But it wasn't there this time. All that was there was shock.

❧ 10 ❧

A SUSPECT

"How did he get mud on him?" Bea asked.

"It's not just *on* him. It's *in* him," Blake replied as if he were giving the time.

"*What?*" I shouted getting the attention of the entire café. "Sorry. Just heard they were changing the name of the Big Mac." I waved. Everyone went back to what they were doing.

When I pulled myself together, I looked at Blake, who had the tiniest smirk on his stoic face.

I would like to just state for the record that I didn't think I'd ever seen Blake laugh out loud. He'd never burst out laughing, chuckled, guffawed, or giggled in my presence. So to see even this tiny sliver of a grin made me feel as if he had caught a glimpse of me in my underwear. He looked really handsome too. I hated it. I knew I flushed a hundred shades of embarrassed. I just knew I did.

"The coroner removed a good bit of mud from his mouth and throat," Jake said, paying more attention to Bea's reaction than the rest of us.

"Someone who decided to be so creative had to leave fingerprints," Aunt Astrid said. "Did you find any?"

"Nope. Not a one. There was some mud in the house." Jake shrugged. "We are at a real loss for this one. And unfortunately, Niles wasn't that nice of a guy to everyone he did business with, so we've got a suspect list a mile long. That's what brings us here." Jake looked at my aunt with the saddest puppy-dog eyes I'd ever seen. "Aunt Astrid, I have to ask you a couple questions."

My aunt stiffened in her seat.

"Am I a suspect?"

"Your name came up a few times. This is just routine. We have to do it," Jake said sadly. "Believe me when I tell you I'm more embarrassed about this than anything."

"It's all right, Jake. I have nothing to hide." She

tugged at the neckline of her blouse. My aunt was a full-figured woman. She wore wonderfully flowing, bohemian-style clothes that made her look like a gypsy. Her dishwater blonde hair was streaked with naturally silver strands. Anyone who looked at her but didn't know her would think she was an artist of some kind. A person dedicated to creating and embellishing. Never someone who destroyed or hurt, let alone killed.

"Why don't we go talk in the back?" she said as she slowly ambled toward her tarot-reading table in the back of the café. Jake followed her with his notepad and a pencil in his hand. Blake stayed at the counter.

"Is that really necessary?" I asked. "You know as well as we do that Aunt Astrid had nothing to do with Niles's death."

"We have to leave our feelings out of it, Cath. Better to follow procedure and be wrong than to manipulate it and miss something."

"You sound like an overgrown Boy Scout reciting his pledge."

"The Boy Scout pledge is *always be prepared*. That's slightly different from what Jake and I are doing." He looked at me while he took a sip of his coffee.

"You know, someday, someone is going to mistake your never-ending quest to educate the world as really annoying sarcasm and knock you out."

"Cath." Bea took hold of my arm. "Blake is right. I don't like it either. But Mom is in the clear. We both know that. She would never hurt anyone."

I looked at Blake. How he could sit there so calmly while his partner interrogated my aunt for a murder everyone knew she didn't commit was a mystery to me. Yet there he was, sipping his coffee as if it were any other day.

Jake and Aunt Astrid were in the back for over half an hour. When they finally came back to the front of the café, Aunt Astrid looked fine, but Jake was green and clammy.

"What's wrong with you?" Bea asked. "Do you want me to take you home?"

"No. I'm fine. I'll see you tonight." Without waiting for his usual kiss, Jake tucked the file folder underneath his arm and left.

"What do I owe you for the coffee, Bea?" Blake asked, standing quickly.

"Nothing, Blake." Bea waved him away as if shooing a fly. "You guys be careful out there."

Bea's voice was soft with worry. She watched as Blake hurried after Jake.

"What happened back there?" I asked my aunt.

"You know. Just like you see on television. Where were you on such-and-such a date? How did you know the victim? Did you ever have any conflicts, issues, or arguments?" She shrugged and smiled. "It really wasn't that bad. Except that I don't have an alibi."

We all just sort of stood there.

"What does that mean?" Bea asked.

"It means I said I was home by myself, but no one can verify I was there the whole night. I've had words with Niles, and we weren't on very good terms. It looks a little suspicious. That's all."

"But Jake won't arrest you," I said. "You're family. He wouldn't do that after everything we've all been through. Hell, even if you did…" My mouth stopped moving, and I just sort of let it hang there.

"Look." My aunt's voice was firm. "We can't blame Jake for doing his job. Bea, don't take this out on him. He's a good cop. A good detective. I have faith in his skills, even if all the evidence is pointing at me for the moment."

I wanted to close up the café, go down in the

bunker with Bea and Aunt Astrid, and start some real digging on Niles's case.

The bunker was discovered after the Brew-Ha-Ha almost burned down. It was just a simple cement cellar that we used for a meeting place when none of us wanted to go home. There was a comfy old sofa and a couple of tables. I made sure a nice stash of Oreo cookies, juice boxes, and a few other odds and ends were stocked down there. It was a safe place. No one knew about it but Bea, Aunt Astrid, and me.

That was part of the reason why I wanted to go down there. The other reason was I really wanted to hide. I wanted to hide from this horrible turn of events that had unfurled so far. But I also wanted to hide from Tom and his mother.

There couldn't be a more inconvenient time to meet. I looked at the clock and wondered if I should call him and see if rescheduling was possible. What would I tell him? *Sorry, Tom and Mrs. Warner, but my aunt is suspected of a really grisly murder. Can we have dinner some other time?*

Yikes. That was worse than a fib that my stomach was acting up.

No. I wasn't going to cancel dinner. I'd go. Hopefully the change of scenery and the lively conversation would be as good as a rest. Maybe I'd come back feeling refreshed and ready to deal with this new situation.

"I don't want you girls to worry" was the last thing Aunt Astrid said.

Still, throughout the day, I waffled on whether or not to go. Finally, it got to a point when it was too late to change my mind even if I wanted to.

11

PSYCHIC VIBES

"Aren't you going to go get changed?" my aunt asked me as I was wiping down the counter. "Didn't you bring a change of clothes with you?"

"I did," I said. Just as I was about to say I wasn't going, Treacle slunk into the room from the kitchen. He wasn't the only one who could read my thoughts.

"You haven't been yourself all day," my aunt whispered.

"I'm worried." I shrugged. "Innocent people have gone to jail before."

"You and Bea need to give our fine detectives some credit. They are in the early stages of this investigation. I'm sure I'm not the only one whose story is slightly transparent."

I didn't know what else to say.

"Cath, go get ready. You are meeting Tom's mother."

"Are you sure?"

"Your cousin is going to have me over for dinner. Jake will need to be soothed because, like you, he's worried. Except he's worried about looking like the bad guy." She tilted her head. "Once I calm the two of them down, we will probably talk about you for the rest of the night until you get home."

Funny. That was exactly what I'd be doing too. Treacle jumped up on Aunt Astrid's favorite table for two and proceeded to curl up on all of her receipts.

"Okay," I mumbled.

I had decided to keep the outfit simple, and I was really glad I had done so. Unlike my cousin, who could get picked up by a twister, swirled around a couple hundred times, and dropped in a muddy field and still look like a fashion model, I had a little more work to do.

When I stepped out of the bathroom after changing into a tan pencil skirt and a flowery red-and-white blouse, I wasn't feeling any more confident.

"You look so cute!" Bea gushed, running over to me. "Where did you get that blouse?"

"Thrift store," I said while I smoothed it across my stomach. "It's not too much? Too bright?"

"No. It's just perfect for almost summer."

We had finished decorating the café the same day Tom invited me out. Streamers hung from the ceiling. Not only were there adorable vintage Independence Day statues of Uncle Sam, but each and every branch of the military was also represented, and there were different variations of Old Glory and even red and blue votive candles on the tables.

Now that I was taking a minute to slow down, I looked around and thought the place really looked beautiful. There was no way Tom's mother wouldn't like it.

"Now, remember." Aunt Astrid smoothed my hair back over my shoulders and looked me in the eyes. "Be yourself."

"And if you can't be yourself, be Batman," Bea piped up as she stroked Treacle. "Batman is always cool."

"That's helpful." I smirked.

Before I could go back to the bathroom and give myself one more look-over, I saw Tom walk past the window. The woman with him was not anything like I'd pictured.

After he said she'd just gotten back home from

Europe, I expected to see a svelte, cosmopolitan-looking woman in a designer dress, maybe even a hat, with loads of makeup that looked professionally applied, and a long neck like Audrey Hepburn.

Instead, she was a Dolly Parton look-alike with a full figure and red cowboy boots. Her nails were bright red and matched her lipstick.

When she smiled, I saw where Tom had gotten his dimples.

They were chatting pleasantly as they walked in. Let's just say I expected Bea and my aunt to go over the woman with a fine-tooth comb. What I didn't expect was the response I got from Treacle.

He sat up on the table and watched Tom intently as he introduced his mother to Bea and Aunt Astrid first.

"And this is Cath," he said proudly. "Cath, this is my mom. Patience Warner."

"Hi, Patience." I reached out my hand to her.

"Cath, it is really nice to finally meet you. Tom has told me so much about you. I feel I know you and your family already."

"She's very suspicious," Treacle said.

"Tom said you just got back from Europe. That had to be nice."

Patience waved her hand as if her trip was the

last thing she wanted to talk about. Who in their right mind would want to discuss spending almost a year traveling, right? Boring.

"She's sizing you up, Cath," Treacle said. *"She's sizing you up like Aunt Astrid is sizing her up."*

I looked at my aunt, who had an expression as if she were trying to solve an algebra problem in her head.

"Well, I don't know about you ladies, but I am starving," Tom said. "Are you ready to go?"

"I'm hungry," I said. It was true. I realized just then that I hadn't had so much as a cupcake all day. There was so much going on that I had literally forgotten to eat. For me to forget to eat was really saying something.

I stroked Treacle, who gave me his warning one more time, hugged my aunt, and gave a high five to Bea, who winked before turning to ring up a customer.

"That's a quaint little café. How long have you worked there?" Patience asked.

"Forever," I said proudly. "My aunt owns it. Bea is her daughter. We grew up like sisters."

She continued to ask a lot of questions. Where I lived. Where were my parents? Where did I go to school? Did I have any siblings other than Bea?

Taking everything Bea and Aunt Astrid had said into consideration, I assumed that Patience was just nervous. This was her way of ensuring there was no awkward silences, no questions drifting off in weird directions.

When we arrived at Tito's Mexican Bar and Grill, I did my best to try to ask her questions about her, but she didn't seem too interested in answering anything personal. Once we all sat down and the smell of food hit my stomach, I threw all caution to the wind.

"Tom, did you hear about the suspicious death in town? Niles Freudenfur. He was a con-artist psychic. They found him dead in his house."

I didn't know what prompted me to spill my guts the way I did. But by the time I realized what I was talking about, it was too late to take any of it back. I told him how long he had lain dead before his body was discovered, how he had a creepy doll room, and how people weren't buying his stuff at the estate sale.

"Is that something you'll be working on, Tom?" his mother asked nervously.

"That's not in my jurisdiction. If they need additional man power, they'll call some of us boys in, but most of the time, our departments don't mix."

"I can see why my son likes you, Cath."

The statement caught me off guard.

"You both like the more gruesome aspects of life."

"I don't like gruesome things," I replied. "It's just something that happened in town. Normally, Wonder Falls is pretty quiet. Boring, even."

"Mom. Really?"

"I just don't know where you get it." Patience smiled, but there was something underneath it. I was sure she didn't like me. That had to be it. She thought I was a weirdo.

"My mom worries," Tom said as he patted the older woman's hand. "She thinks I am up to my eyeballs in cadavers and criminals all day long."

"Oh, Patience, Wonder Falls is a great place to be a police officer. It is very quiet around here. In fact, Bea's husband, Jake, is a detective. He's on the Freudenfur case, and they are narrowing down the suspects."

There were a slew of words that hung in my throat. Luckily I pulled them down, swallowing hard, and didn't say a word about Aunt Astrid being suspected in Niles's death. It wasn't true, so why go spreading rumors as if it might be? Better to laugh about the whole crazy notion once the real culprit was caught. More importantly, I didn't want to give Patience the idea her son was hanging around some mutant killer family.

But I could tell the damage was already done. Patience gave me that smile-smirk people gave when they didn't want to be outright rude and scowl at you. I was not the right girl for her son. Part of me, a really tiny part, maybe down by my pinky toe, was feeling the same way.

The funny thing was that I had expected to hear stories about Tom as a kid. Things he said as a little boy or stuff he did at school. Normal things that parents always brought up to embarrass their grown children a little.

My aunt loved to tell the story about me when I was five or six and found a toad. She and my mother had taken Bea and me out to some nature preserve. There were tiny little pockets of water, so of course there were toads.

I strolled up to my mother and aunt and showed them the big, roly-poly thing that sat uncomfortably in my little hands, one of its legs dangling down with its hands tucked underneath it. When I first spied it, it was so dark in color I thought it was just a clump of dirt. Its skin was bumpy and a rich, thick dark brown, almost black color. The thing's glassy black eyes barely blinked.

"Now, Cath. Be careful. If you kiss that toad, he might become a prince," my mom said.

"Not this one," I had to argue back.

"Why not that one? How do you know?" Aunt Astrid asked me very seriously.

"Tried it already. He just stayed a toad."

That story sent my aunt over the moon every time she repeated it. I really didn't know what was so funny. But that didn't matter. It tickled her, so she'd tell it every chance she got.

But Patience didn't tell stories like that. She talked about her friends in Europe. She mentioned a few things about Tom's father, but he had passed away. But mostly she spoke about her other two children. Tom had a sister in Kansas who was married to a doctor. He had an older brother who lived in Maine and had married a lawyer.

I had no idea what Tom's siblings did for a living, but I could see the pattern here. I wasn't sure what I could have done. The doctor and lawyer slots were already filled. Maybe she would have liked it if Tom were dating a politician or maybe an heiress to some frozen-dessert fortune. But a girl who worked at her aunt's café wasn't going to cut it.

I didn't think the fact that I could communicate with animals would have impressed her much, either.

Patience Warner would probably be very good friends with Dolores Eversol. She wasn't quite the blowhard Dolores was, but I could see her desire for bragging rights was pretty strong.

I remembered what my aunt said about just being myself. Even if I tried, I couldn't put on airs. I loved my family and was proud of them no matter what. Even if my aunt had stumbled into a fugue state and made Niles Freudenfur a human mud pie, I would still love her. And Bea, well, what wasn't there to love about Bea?

So I jumped in feet first, surprising Tom and Patience as well as myself.

"Patience, do you believe in the paranormal?"

Tom blinked. I couldn't tell by his smirk if he approved or didn't.

"It's kind of a hobby of mine," I continued. "This murder that just happened. The guy was supposed to be a clairvoyant. Do you think a person can have those kinds of powers to see the future?"

"I'm not sure. I suppose anything is possible. But if the man could really see the future, how come he didn't know someone was coming to kill him?"

"That's a good point." I chuckled.

The table was quiet.

"I've heard that people who see ghosts in a specific area, that area is often the same place UFOs are sighted. I've never been sure what the correlation between the two is, but it's a fascinating connection."

"I've never seen a ghost or a UFO," Patience said.

"What about that one time?" Tom interrupted.

"What time?"

"That time you said you were having your fortune told with Kaye and her father was there. Back when you were teenagers." Tom looked at me. "She said the lady doing their fortunes predicted something that made Kaye start crying."

"We don't need to talk about that," Patience said.

"Come on, Mom. Don't you think I'm old enough to hear it? I promise I won't have to sleep with the light on or come in your bed." Tom turned to me. "I used to do that when I'd watch scary movies as a kid. That was my promise."

"Honey, would you get the check, please?" his mother asked firmly.

I waited a couple seconds, but it was obvious Patience wasn't going to share this story of her psychic reading. She looked at her watch and commented on how late it was.

"Would you like to come back to the café for a coffee?" I asked, finally feeling like myself.

"I don't drink coffee after three o'clock," Patience said.

"We have wonderful chamomile tea. Bea puts this honey infused with lavender in it. Even I have to admit it tastes good."

"No, thank you. Not tonight."

I did my best. I really did try. I didn't mean to go off on tangents about crime scenes, and I thought my toad story was a big hit. But I couldn't say I learned anything about Tom that I didn't already know, and his mom was locked up tighter than a clamshell.

By the time I got home, it was still fairly early.

Tom walked me to the door and told me he'd call me the next day. I got a peck on the cheek and an awkward hug good-bye. For the first time since I met him, I was glad Tom was gone.

"Thank goodness you are safe." Treacle came from his hiding spot among the shrubs.

"She's just a peculiar lady. I think she's harmless."

"I don't know. The psychic vibes were so strong my fur was standing on edge. She was up to something."

"Do you think she was a psychic?"

"*Most definitely.*"

I scooped Treacle up and went to my aunt's house. If anyone would give it to me straight, it would be her. I had to know what her impression of Patience was.

12

BLOODY TOOTH

"Sort of an early evening, isn't it?" Aunt Astrid asked.

Marshmallow was slinking around her ankles then came and gave me an affectionate rub. Peanut Butter was chasing her tail in the hall behind my aunt.

"Yeah. I was myself. I guess that is what did it." I shrugged.

Treacle leaped from my arms and gave Marshmallow a head butt before they both retreated to the nearest armchair to sleep. Peanut Butter was not through teaching her tail a lesson.

"No, no, honey." My aunt gave me a big hug as she pulled me into the house. "Bea is here. She's worried about you—and me."

"Oh, I'm not in any danger of going to the pokey like you are," I joked. "I'm just a misfit destined to grow old with my cat."

"*That sounds like heaven,*" Treacle said as he yawned then curled up into a ball.

"*Yeah it does,*" I replied, smiling at him.

"So?" I said as I walked into the living room, which blended into the kitchen.

Bea was standing at the counter with a cup of tea.

"What did you think of Mrs. Patience Warner?" I asked.

"It isn't up to us to tell you who to like and who not to like," Bea replied.

"I didn't like her," I said. "No. I guess I liked her fine if I had just met her, and she was having coffee at the café. But as Tom's mom, I don't think it's a good fit."

Retelling the events of the evening made me cringe.

"I really did just try to be myself. Patience didn't seem impressed."

Bea looked at my aunt, and I could tell they had something on their minds.

"Okay. Spill it," I said.

"Patience had the aura of a clairvoyant," Bea said.

"She also had some psychic scars, as she has

probably fought to subdue what comes naturally to her," Aunt Astrid said. "She's used her gift a couple of times but for the wrong reasons. So now it terrifies her. From what I could see, she has it locked up tight."

"What do you mean?" I scratched my head. "I brought up the whole paranormal thing to see what she'd say, and she didn't seem interested at all."

"Her gift, whatever it is, has something to do with Tom. There was a definite connection between the two of them," Aunt Astrid said.

"Tom said he has had some visions and gut feelings in the past. He told me that early on when we first started dating," I said. "If I remember right, he said his family had a little bit of the magic running through it. Not like us, of course. But I took it to sound as if they at least respected it. That doesn't seem to be the case."

"Without sitting down with her and getting a real reading, I can't say what her true feelings are," Aunt Astrid said.

"Don't forget, Cath, she was meeting you for the first time too. Tom will always be her son. Some mothers can be very territorial."

"Yeah, well, I don't think my describing the crime scene at Niles's house helped my cause any."

"Was Tom interested?"

"I don't know. I was rambling. The whole night is a blur I'd rather forget."

"I think we could all use a distraction." My aunt walked into the kitchen, pushing Bea out of the way in order to get into a cabinet. She stood up, holding a flashlight. "Who wants to go on an adventure?"

Within minutes, my aunt, the three cats, Bea, and I were piled into Bea's car and cruising at a whopping twenty-five miles an hour down the road in the direction of Niles's house.

"Bea, the speed limit is thirty-five. You can do forty," I urged.

"How would that look? The wife of Detective Jake Johnson gets pulled over for speeding with his mother-in-law, a cousin, and three cats in the car," she replied, gripping the wheel tighter in defiance. "A fast drive could be your last drive."

"How could I be related to such a geek?" I asked.

"I ask myself that all the time," Bea snapped back. "Now stop making me angry. Would you like to walk?"

"Yes, I'd like to get there tonight," I teased back. "Tell you what. Let me out to walk, and I'll let you know what's going on since I'll get there before you."

Bea was getting more and more annoyed with me as we drove. But I could hear my aunt giggling in the back seat. Finally, we made it to Niles's house.

"I don't think we should park in the driveway or on the street," Bea said.

"You're right, honey. Let's cruise around and see what we can find."

As luck would have it, just two blocks down, someone was having a party.

"Hey, just pull up there behind those cars. No one will notice us," I said.

With the car safely camouflaged in the long line of cars along the street, we all piled out, cats included, and began to walk toward the house.

"A car's coming." I pointed ahead.

Quickly, we dashed into the tall brush that flanked the sides of the road. Within seconds, the car whizzed by.

"I think we'd better stay hidden," my aunt suggested. "After Jake's interview and the allegations made, I don't think it would be good for anyone to see us sneaking around the property of the murder victim."

Bea and I agreed. So I instructed the cats to lead the way since they could see so much better than we could. Before long, we could see the house looming ahead of us.

Aunt Astrid snapped on her flashlight, confident no one could see us either from the road or from the neighboring houses.

"How many acres did he own?" I asked.

"Ten," Bea answered. "But I don't think he probably ventured out in the farther corners very much at his age."

"You don't think so?" Aunt Astrid pointed with her flashlight. "Then what is that?"

Ahead of us about thirty feet was a makeshift stone altar with weird trinkets scattered all around it. It was partially hidden by wild vegetation.

"Oh snap," I whispered.

The cats did not go to investigate the platform. In fact, they proceeded past it rather quickly, looking at it suspiciously as if something might suddenly move.

There were two crystal balls on a giant flat rock that was balancing on a smaller flat rock. A brass sound bowl was also there.

"Is this anything used in *The Sequence of Ursaken*?"

"It's hard to tell," my aunt said as she approached the site. "It looks like it could fit several different ceremonies. But here is a sure sign of a rookie." She pointed to the top of the altar. "A pentagram."

"You're kidding!" Bea huffed. From FBI profilers to teenagers looking to upset their parents, the pentagram had been used to indicate satanic rituals and properties. The truth was that a much more elaborate star diagram was used to summon the prince of darkness. Whatever Niles was hoping to bring forth could have been anybody's guess. But the chances were pretty slim of anything using this poorly designed pentagram to punch a hole into this world.

"I'm seeing an overlap, though," Aunt Astrid said as she moved her arms as if she were swimming underwater. "This was hidden."

"What do you mean?" Bea asked.

"I'm sure the police looked over the property after they found Niles. Unless they are hiding this fact from the public, I'd have to say this was camouflaged." My aunt continued to push things aside like curtains. Just as she was about to turn around, both crystal balls started to glow.

"What's causing that?" I asked. Just because we were witches and familiar with crystal balls didn't mean we didn't freak out when they started to glow without any provocation.

"I don't sense anything," Bea replied. "And I mean literally. I don't sense *anything*."

I listened and didn't hear any bugs or nighttime birds. The only rustling was the cats carefully skulking through the brush toward the house.

This had happened to me once before. All the normal sounds of life stopped, and it was as though I were in a bubble. It was quiet like that, only I didn't feel as if I were in a bubble. I felt as though the rest of the earth had vanished and left us as the only things left alive on this tiny square of property.

"Let's get closer to the house," Aunt Astrid suggested.

"How are you guys doing?" I asked the cats.

They skittered ahead a couple paces then stopped and looked around. After a sniff of the air, they looked at each other but said nothing.

"Treacle? You sense something?"

He turned around and looked at me.

"Something is in the ground."

"What?"

"Something is in the ground."

"Do you mean like the ground is cursed or…"

"No. There is something in it. Something that isn't happy."

I repeated that to Aunt Astrid and Bea. We all looked down at the ground. I don't know why. What were we expecting to see? My first thought was mounds of dirt moving up and down as if it were breathing. Maybe a gruesome hand digging its way out from an unmarked grave or something to that effect. All I saw was grass and weeds and strange stones and lawn ornaments leading up to the house.

"Should we go back?"

"Let's just get a little closer," Aunt Astrid whispered. "I want to look inside the house. Just one quick peek."

We all agreed to keep going, but I was getting a strange feeling, as if the back end of the property were closing in on us. I kept looking back over my shoulder, expecting there to be a huge wall of bushes coming closer and closer while beyond the wall would be pitch blackness. But each time, I just saw the same scenery we had passed and the nighttime sky with plenty of stars and clouds hanging silently in heaven. The crystal balls were glowing a sickly color, as if they were cataract eyes staring ahead blindly.

They seemed to follow as we made our way closer to the house. Finally, we reached what I'd say was the actual backyard. There were a lot more lawn decorations and concrete benches. But it was obvious from the overgrowth that Niles hadn't hired a landscaper to maintain his property.

I had looked out the kitchen window at the estate sale, and I remembered there being some kind of pond near the back of the house. But the windows were so dirty I couldn't make out exactly where it was or see the vegetation growing around it.

Bea gasped. "What is that?"

Aunt Astrid shined the light where Bea was pointing. All along the base of several strange rocks were what looked like bloody pieces of flesh.

"Oh my gosh." I moaned. "We're too late. Someone else has been killed here. And from the looks of it, they were dismembered too."

Aunt Astrid slowly crept up to the bloody red thing and inhaled deeply.

"Strawberries," she muttered.

"What?" Bea and I said in unison.

"This isn't bloody body parts. It is a fungus called Bleeding Tooth. Or if you want to get technical, *hydnellum peckii*. It smells like fresh strawberries but is deadly poisonous."

"Who would have such a thing growing in their yard?" Bea shivered.

"The same kind of person who would have those creepy plants and those creepy plants." I directed Aunt Astrid's light to what looked like a bed of Venus flytrap types of sprouts and some purple hanging vegetation that looked like tentacles.

"You know what this is?" I stood straight up proudly. "This is an H.P. Lovecraft garden."

"A what?" Now it was Bea and Aunt Astrid's turn to sound off in unison.

"You know the author H.P. Lovecraft? He wrote all those stories about monsters so ugly they couldn't be described and creatures with thousands of tentacles and eyes and stuff."

Both of them looked at me as if I had just admitted to licking toads.

"Anyway, I saw in a magazine. If you wanted to move away from a traditional flower garden, you could have an H.P. Lovecraft garden. It included Venus flytraps, weird-looking orchids, poisonous white oleander... things like this that are flowers but they look like tentacles."

Still, my family looked at me as though I'd sprouted a third eye in the middle of my forehead.

"I'm not saying it's what I'd want. I'm just saying it's a *thing*."

"What kind of magazines are you reading?" Bea asked.

"The kind that help when we are trespassing on a crime scene," I replied.

"Did you read anything about strange foot-prints?" Aunt Astrid interrupted our tiff by elbowing us both and pointing her flashlight beam at the ground to the left of us.

They were thick, muddy footprints that were slightly larger than a normal man's feet.

"Was there anything like this in Jake's file?" I looked at Bea.

"I don't remember seeing anything like this." She pointed. "But look where they are coming from."

"That can't be," I whispered.

"I'm seeing it, but I don't believe it," Aunt Astrid said as she kept shining her light on the footprints, which looked as if they came out of the slimy, over-grown, dilapidated pond that sat pitifully neglected in the middle of the yard.

"It's an optical illusion," I said. "The other foot-steps got washed away. As simple as that." I couldn't imagine a man submerging himself in that scummy water for any amount of time in order to ambush Niles Freudenfur. Stagnant, sitting water was a cornucopia of mosquito eggs and scorpion flies and tadpoles, and those were just the critters you could see. That didn't count the world of bacteria that was invisible to the naked eye. No. Even in a full hazmat body suit, there would be some skin exposed that could absorb some kind of creepy crawly.

"No one in their right mind would go in that water." I shivered at the thought.

We were all stumped as we tried to figure how these footprints got there when we heard a sound that was not of this earth.

The cats, who had been sneaking around and doing their own investigating, darted back to us. I had never heard a sound like that before.

"Aunt Astrid," I whispered, "tell me you know what that sound is."

She just shook her head.

"Bea, can you tell where it's coming from?"

There was no answer.

"Bea?" I took Aunt Astrid's hand with the flashlight and shined it toward my cousin. She was standing there crying. Her entire body was shaking.

"There's nothing there," she whimpered. "Nothing at all. Just void."

"We've got to get her out of here," I said.

"Yes." Aunt Astrid took Bea's hand.

"Treacle. Can you guys lead us out of here?"

"We can't go back the way we came."

"Why not?"

"It isn't there."

"*What do you mean, 'It isn't there'?*"

"*We have to go around to the front of the house. There is no other way.*"

"*Fine. You lead. We'll follow.*"

I grabbed my aunt's other hand as she pulled Bea behind her.

The scream was an angry, guttural sound as if it were being ripped from the lungs of a creature. It wasn't human. It wasn't an animal. At least not any kind of animal I'd ever heard before. It vibrated down to my core, making me tremble too. But I didn't let go of Aunt Astrid.

The cats were moving faster and faster until we wove our way around the house. The shrubs and trees and foliage reached out as if they were trying to trip us. I knew that wasn't really happening. I knew that because we were all panicked we were losing our footing. It was too dark to see anything, so our other senses were heightened. We heard the screams. Whatever it was behind us was gaining.

"I see the street!" I shouted, pointing.

I heard Bea crying. Aunt Astrid wasn't making a sound. I could only hear my own panting in my ears as we hurried to the safety of the road.

When we finally reached it, we slowed down to catch our breath.

"*Don't stop!*" Treacle, Peanut Butter, and Marshmallow all cried. "*Keep moving! We aren't safe yet!*"

"But we're away from the house. We're on the street," I gasped.

"*Run!*"

Without letting go of Aunt Astrid's hand, I pulled them along.

"*We have to hurry! We aren't safe yet!*"

It felt as if it were taking forever. Bea's car was still where we left it at the end of the line of cars. Finally, I could hear music and people talking where the party was coming from. But as I started to slow down and listen, I realized it wasn't a normal party. The voices spoke quickly and in a sort of hissing chant. We couldn't see them, but we heard them.

"There they are."

"They are liars."

"Get them quickly."

"It will get them."

"Golem will get them."

"Get them."

"Get the liars."

"Golem. Golem. Golem."

We were nowhere out of the woods yet.

"Bea, can you drive?" She looked at me with wild eyes. "Bea! Drive the car!"

She nodded, wiping her eyes and letting go of her mother's hand. She dashed to the driver's side and climbed in. All the cats jumped in the back seat. I practically shoved Aunt Astrid in as if she were the victim of a kidnapping. When I was finally in the front seat, I slammed the door, pressed the lock, and looked at my cousin.

"Punch it, Bea!"

We peeled out of there at about five miles an hour, made sure to signal getting onto the road, and stopped for two seconds at the stop sign at the corner.

Still, we made it. Slowly but surely, we made it off Niles's property and in one piece.

Aunt Astrid finally spoke. "What was making that noise?"

"Nothing," Bea answered. "It was pure nothing making that noise."

13

TREASURE CHEST ESTATE SALES

The next day, none of us were in good shape for work at the café. It was a magic hangover without the benefit of enjoying the magic.

"What did we do last night?" I grumbled as I rubbed my temples. "I feel like something the cat dragged in."

"He *did* drag you in," Bea joked, wincing at her own headache. "I saw poor Treacle leading you in by the cuff of your shirt."

Aunt Astrid came from the kitchen, carrying a fizzing glass of Alka-Seltzer.

"Hello, honey." She patted me on the back as she scooted tenderly behind her favorite table and took a seat. Before the fizzing in her glass totally stopped, she drank the concoction down.

"What do you think made that noise last night?" I asked.

"Which noise?" Bea said. "The screaming banshee noise or the hundreds of vulgar taunts coming from the party noise?"

"That wasn't from the party. It only seemed like it was from that party," Aunt Astrid whispered with squinted eyes. It was obvious her head was hurting too.

"If other people are hearing this stuff, you'd think the police would have been called a couple dozen times," Bea said. "I know for a fact that Jake hasn't heard anything about disturbances over there. In fact, the only reason anyone called the cops for a wellness check on Niles was because no one had seen or heard from him in a couple weeks."

"How is Jake?" Aunt Astrid asked, tilting her head to the right. "I do hope he knows that I don't blame him for doing his job."

"He's pretty broken up about it. He hates that he's got to keep you on the list because you don't have an alibi." Bea pouted. "But he knows the truth, Mom."

"I know he does."

"Does anyone think it would be a good idea to pay a visit to Dolores Eversol?" I pounded my fist into my palm.

"Now Cath, you know I'd never want you to physically hurt anyone," Aunt Astrid said. "I appreciate your desire to avenge me, but getting yourself thrown in jail won't do any of us any good."

"I wasn't talking about getting physical. I can't throw a punch. I just thought maybe we could go over there and hurl insults at her house. Maybe be really, really sarcastic at her."

"That sounds like fun." Bea nodded.

"No. We don't even know if she's the one who told Jake anything. Just let her alone. She's obviously a lost soul." My aunt rubbed her temple.

"Hey, can we make a group decision on something?" I asked seriously. "If we have to travel to any suspicious location where there could be bodily, mental, or spiritual harm done to one or all of us, I drive? Can we all agree on that?"

"I got us out of there. My cousin thinks she's an Andretti and this is Indianapolis," she said to the customer in front of her who had ordered a coffee.

The bald man, who'd been in the café a few times before, smiled at her. Of course he did. All the fellows smiled at Bea.

"I'm just saying that from now on, I should be the designated driver."

"But your car is so small," Bea complained.

"How much room do you need to escape with your life, hmm? Want to tell me that? I'd like to know."

"We made it without so much as a scratch."

"This time." I bumped her with my hip as I grabbed two giant oatmeal cookies and one sugar cookie for the next customer.

Once the counter was empty, we got more serious.

"I'll tell you what," I said. "I didn't pick up on any animals in the area at all except the cats. That's pretty rare. In fact, I'd say that never happens."

"I didn't feel anything either," Bea said. "It was the most terrifying feeling of my life because it was like a black hole. There was no aura, no soul or essence. It was just a void."

"Yet we all heard that scream," Aunt Astrid said. "And we all heard the weird voices. They seemed to be coming from the party. The scream was definitely coming from the property."

"That book you bought at the estate sale... did Niles mark anything from it? The diary. Did you finish reading it? Does it say anything that might help us figure out exactly what we are dealing with?" Bea wiped off the counter as she spoke.

"No. There was not much in there. I sure would like to get a look at the books Jake and Blake collected. That might help us out a good deal."

"I'll talk to Jake, but..." Bea shrugged.

"No. He can't know. If anyone gets wind that he is helping a suspect in a murder because of his personal ties, it could ruin his career and my chance to clear my name." Aunt Astrid shook her head. "I can't think while my head is pounding. Let's just try to make it through today. Hopefully, tomorrow we'll all be feeling better."

"I wonder if what we are feeling is why no one was buying any of Niles's things," I said. "We've got the additional burden of heightened psychic or tele-kinetic senses, but regular people were probably just getting creeped out."

"That could be," my aunt answered.

"I wonder how the rest of the sale turned out," I mused. In the back of my mind, I remembered talking with Dot, the estate sale coordinator. She was there in the house all day. I wondered if she'd heard anything at all while she was working.

The business card she'd given me was still in the back pocket of my jeans. I pulled it out and looked at the name: Dorothy "Dot" McGill. Estate Sale Coordinator. Treasure Chest Estate Sales.

Since Bea had to worry about Jake, and Aunt Astrid had to worry about herself, I felt it was up to me. Besides, anything that kept my mind off the terrible meeting of *the mother* was welcomed.

We had a fairly busy day at the café. Thankfully, by quitting time, we were all feeling much better. At lunchtime, Aunt Astrid stuck with the Alka-Seltzer, and Bea drank so much tea her eyes were floating. I went and got a hamburger down the street, and it cured me almost instantly. While I was out, I also put a call in to Dot. Maybe she'd tell me if she had encountered anything weird while at Niles's house.

"Oh yes. I remember you. You bought the bookcase."

"That's right," I said.

"How's it working out for you?"

"It looks just perfect. I needed something to brighten up a dreary corner, and it did just the trick."

"That's great. What can I do for you?"

"Well, I've got a strange request."

Without giving away everything we had learned over the past couple of days, I inquired about the sales.

"A friend of mine was at the house and said she

had a weird feeling about the whole house and that was why she didn't buy anything. Did you feel any kind of strange sensations? Vibes? Anything?"

"You know, it's funny you should say that," Dot replied.

My heart jumped.

"When we first got to the house, we had to do a survey of everything."

She mentioned going out into the backyard and considering including some of the lawn decorations.

"I think they were anchored in the ground. If there was ever a tornado, those suckers weren't going to budge." She chuckled. "But the really strange thing was the body shape dug in the ground."

"The what?"

"It was the strangest thing I ever saw. You know how when we were kids and it snowed, we'd go out, fall on our backs in the snow, and make snow angels?"

"Sure I do."

"Well, this was like someone fell in the mud and left a perfect imprint of the body going down about four feet."

"In the mud?"

"Yup. I had one of my guys fill it up with dirt and

make it look like someone had been digging but hadn't finished the project. It was creepy."

"I'll bet." I wrote down what Dot was telling me.

"And you went upstairs, so you saw the doll room. That was enough to make me throw back a double shot after work. Even though I have to admit that many men like Mr. Freudenfur have doll collections."

"What do you mean?"

"You know, guys who prefer to be more feminine. I'm not very PC. But you know what I mean."

"They have doll collections?"

"Many of them do. I think it stems from their childhood. But I'm no shrink. Just an estate sale coordinator."

"Did any of the dolls sell?"

"No. We ended up donating them to Macey's Resale Shop. They were happy to have them along with the other things that didn't sell. The entire endeavor was a bust."

"Dot, I don't want to keep you any longer, but can I ask who contacted you to organize the sale? It couldn't have been Niles." I laughed, uncomfortable.

"No, of course not." I could hear her smiling on the other end of the phone. "It was Patrick Fouts. All he did was pay us. He didn't stop in. We didn't meet with him. If it weren't for his payment, the entire sale would have been a big bust. I wouldn't know him if he came up and bit me, but I'm truly thankful for him."

"Why do you think he arranged it that way?"

"He said it was too painful to come back in the house."

I nodded. That was a believable excuse. A sad one too.

"One last thing. Did you or any of your people hear any strange sounds around the house?"

"What? Like creaking floor boards or slamming doors?"

"Anything that you couldn't explain."

"Not that I can recall. But we weren't there at night. I made sure of that. The place was weird enough with the sun shining. I didn't want to be around when the sun went down. Call me crazy, but I believe in the paranormal, and when a person dies alone in a house, there has got to be something left behind."

If only you were Tom's mother, I thought. I thanked Dot and wished her better luck at her next sale. When I hung up, I'd already decided to go to Macey's Resale Shop and see if there was anything we missed.

"It's a complete mess," Jake grumbled when I walked into Bea's house later that evening.

"Hello. Is this a bad time?" I asked before making my way into the kitchen.

"No, honey," Bea called. "Are you hungry?"

"That depends on what you are cooking."

I stepped in and saw Blake was there too. Of course he was. He was Jake's partner, and they were glued at the hip.

She huffed. "It's vegetarian lasagna. One of Jake's favorites." She tousled his hair.

"Oh, so cute. Aren't they cute, Blake? That's cute. Too cute. So darn cute."

Bea stuck her tongue out at me and went back to her oven to check on her meal.

"What's a complete mess?" I said to Jake. "Besides your face, I mean."

Jake gave me that sideways look of annoyance.

"It seems the books we pulled from the Freudenfur crime scene were contaminated," Blake answered.

"Oh no. You mean someone tampered with the evidence?"

"No." Jake shook his head. "He means literally contaminated. There is this brownish green substance that has practically eaten away every book we carried out of the place. We had to get the poison-control people to the station. There were people walking around in hazardous material suits. Biohazard bags were being dumped in a giant waste disposal truck. I was sure Blake and I were going to have to get a Karen Silkwood shower. But thankfully no one thought that was necessary."

"And that isn't all," Blake interrupted. For as aggravated as Jake was, Blake was as calm as a Trappist monk. "We had a fellow come into the station to report a prowler on his property the past couple of days and then asking about Niles and if the house was finally empty. When we asked him why he wanted to know, he said that he'd driven by and seen someone lurking around."

I looked at Bea and held my breath.

"What did he say he saw?" I was ready to deny everything even if the witness said that he saw three women and three cats running for their lives.

"This is good." Jake shook his head. "The guy said he saw a man covered from head to toe in a muddy, sludgy substance and that he was standing in the middle of the yard, just staring at him."

"So what did you tell him?" I let my breath out slowly.

"We told him to quit drinking and that if he came into the police department with another story like that, we were going to throw him in the drunk tank until he dried out." Jake smirked.

"Was he drunk?" I asked.

"We didn't smell any alcohol on him. But he was obviously seeing things."

"Did you get the guy's name?" I was just wondering if maybe it was a client of Niles's or just a passerby.

"Patrick Fouts."

Bea dropped the lid of her pan, making such a clatter that we all jumped.

"You okay, Busy-Bea?" Jake asked.

"My hands are wet," she lied.

The guys didn't seem to notice anything wrong.

Beverly, who had given Aunt Astrid Patrick's name, had said he sounded like someone who held himself in very high regard. But according to Jake's description, he was an annoying, possibly drunk person.

Jake changed the subject. "Hey, Bea said you were meeting Tom's mother yesterday. How did it go?"

I looked at Blake as if I had been hiding something. I wasn't. I just didn't go out of my way to tell him anything about my personal life. He had his chance, but he'd blown it.

Technically, it was his doppelgänger that blew it, but I couldn't go backward. Yes, at one time, I had feelings for Blake. Sometimes, during special occasions like Christmas or Valentine's Day, I might feel a twinge of regret that I hadn't worked harder to get to know him.

But then he would open his mouth and say something so crazy or so emotionless that it would make my skin crawl.

Of course, he wasn't always like that. Sometimes when he decided to rattle off some strange facts or stats, it came across as downright funny. There were times I could never tell if he were really being serious or saying these things just to make me laugh.

The proud part of me said he liked making me

laugh. But the practical side of me always insisted that he was doing it to show how much smarter he was than me. I never had a head for book smarts.

"It was okay, I guess," I replied to Jake's question.

"You guess? Tell me straight, Cath. Was she mean to you? I'll make sure no matter where she goes, she'll be racking up the speeding tickets."

"No." I smiled. "You aren't that kind of cop, Jake. I wouldn't expect you to do that for me. Besides, maybe she was having a bad day. Sometimes you can be excited about something and you get a flat tire or bad hair. Suddenly, that thing you were waiting to do has become a big burden."

"What did she say to you?" Blake asked. He looked as if he really wanted to know. I didn't want to get so far into it with him. So I just repeated the part about the doctor and lawyer spouses.

"I guess working at the Brew-Ha-Ha isn't high-end enough." I shrugged.

"But Tom doesn't have a problem with it at all," Bea said. "He knows what you are and what you are all about, and he accepts it."

"He *did*. I don't know if he still does. Mothers can be very persuasive."

I didn't want to say anything, but Tom had also

said he was going to call me tonight, but he hadn't. Sure, he was a cop, and their hours were not set in stone. But I knew it wasn't because of work.

Right now, Tom was probably sitting with a couple of his buddies, going over our date and saying the exact same things.

"You know, Cath, I'm going to tell you something that might help," Jake said. "You know how Bea worries about me every day when I go out of this house. For years, while I was still beat cop, she fussed over me every morning or every night before I stepped out of the house. What would you do while I was gone, honey?"

"I'd stay busy."

"Right. She'd busy herself with cooking fantastic meals, working at the café, and all her other hobbies until I came home. She is my wife. We've been together for a decade, but she will never know me as long as my mother has. Can you imagine being the mother of a police officer?"

I smiled at Jake. His explanation for Patience's attitude came into clearer focus.

"Every day, she's away from him. She can't let her life stand still, so she goes on her trips and does her shopping and maybe dotes on the other siblings a little more. Not because she really loves them more. But in her way, she wants Tom to leave law enforcement. If he wants the attention she's giving the others, he'll leave law enforcement."

"I don't think Tom will ever do that," I said.

"Probably not. He's a good cop and well respected."

Even Blake nodded at this fact.

"But that won't stop his mother from trying to get him to leave it. Not because she doesn't love him but because she does."

I didn't say anything. But I felt a little bit like dirt.

"Just imagine every day when the phone rings, wondering if this is that call. The one that says her boy has been shot. It would kill her. It would kill any mother."

"Thanks, Jake. Now I feel like a real jerk for complaining." I looked at my cousin's tear-streaked face. "And you made Bea cry. Good going."

Jake looked at Bea, smiled, took her hand, and kissed it.

"I'm just telling you, Cath, to give the woman a break. It isn't you. It's the fact that you accept Tom as a cop. I think you kind of like it that he's a cop. Since you and your cousin are always sticking your noses in police business, it helps to know a few guys on the force."

"I do accept him as a cop," I admitted. "What am I supposed to do? Tell him to change his career for me?"

"If you did, I guarantee his mother would be buying the wedding ring for Tom to give to you."

"Do you think you guys will be getting married?" Blake blurted out.

"No." I shook my head. "There has been no talk about that except from Bea and Aunt Astrid. They talk marriage a lot more than me."

"Aunt Astrid is talking about you getting married to Tom?" Blake looked shocked, as if that was something he'd never expect my aunt to talk about, along with flashing gang signs.

"Actually, now that you mention it, it is really only Bea who is pushing it." I smirked at her.

"I can't help it. You are perfect together. Tom's mom will see how wonderful you are the next time you visit her." Bea snapped her fingers. "In fact, you should make a point to see her, maybe without Tom."

"That would be a nice gesture," Jake said. "Just remember that a mother never stops worrying. Even more so the mother of a cop."

"Thanks, Jake." I gave him a kiss on the cheek. "Maybe I will do that. I could bring her some flowers. The grocery store has beautiful roses this time of year."

Just then, the timer went off for Bea's vegetable lasagna.

Blake helped me set the dishes around the table, which was next to the patio door. I didn't want to talk about Niles Freudenfur anymore until I had Bea alone. So I sat back and listened to the details about another case that Blake and Jake were involved in.

"This was one of those typical robberies gone wrong. But the interesting thing was our suspect is over sixty years old. He's built like Bruce Lee. I mean, there isn't an ounce of fat on his body, and here he is, robbing stores."

"That's motivation to get in shape if I ever heard it." Bea laughed. "When the bad guys are working out more than you, you need to climb aboard the pain train." She poked Jake in the side.

"They caught him carrying three thirty-six-inch televisions from Dave's House of Electronics using nothing more than his hands."

"Did he have Bruce Lee's moves?" I asked.

"Thank goodness, no." Jake laughed. "I'd be in big trouble if he had."

"Do you like Bruce Lee movies?" Blake asked.

"I do. It's a guilty passion. I love kung fu. I just love the stories. I know they are all the same, but they are so much fun."

"I don't think I've ever seen a kung fu movie," Bea piped up.

"Bea only likes a movie if you need a hankie while watching it," I said.

"That's not true." She pouted while pulling aluminum foil off the dish that had been in the oven.

"What's your favorite movie?" I prodded.

"*Steel Magnolias.*"

"Cry-fest. Second favorite?"

"*Fried Green Tomatoes.*"

"Pass the tissues, please!" I laughed. "Okay, when no one is around, what is your favorite movie to watch when you can't sleep?"

She thought for a moment then started to laugh.

"*Little Women.*" She giggled.

"The one with Elizabeth Taylor?" I asked.

"There is no other one."

"Right. Let me just use my sleeve as I try to control the waterworks."

We laughed as we all sat down to eat.

Dinner was fun, but as the guys hung around, I was getting antsy to talk to Bea alone. It was obvious she could sense it. But I didn't really like her method of getting us some privacy.

"Cath needs to talk to me, so if you guys will excuse us," she blurted out.

"About what?" Jake asked, knowing it would make me embarrassed.

"Um… cramps." Bea stuttered.

I glared at her as she grabbed my hand and pulled me upstairs to her bedroom.

"Cramps? That's the best you could do?" I put my hand to my cheek to try to bring the bright-red color down.

"Well, at least you know they won't come up here if they think that is what we are talking about."

My cousin had a point there. So I shrugged then proceeded to tell her what I heard from Dot.

"A form of a man in the dirt? That's weird."

"Have you ever heard of such a thing?" I asked.

"No, but I'll bet Mom has. And how much do you want to bet that it has something to do with *The Sequence of Ursaken*?"

Bea and I talked for a little while longer then decided to call it a night. We'd tell Aunt Astrid what we talked about in the morning. So I gave an awkward farewell to the boys, and wouldn't you know it, Blake decided he was leaving too.

"I'll walk you home," he insisted.

"I'm just across the street."

"Good, then it won't take long." He waved good-bye to Bea and Jake, and before I knew what was happening, he had one hand gently holding my arm, as if I were a perpetrator that he was escorting to the station.

"People are going to think I'm being escorted out of Bea's house. You look like a bouncer removing an unsavory."

"Really? Why don't you stagger a little like you're drunk? Shout out a few curse words. Give the neighbors a show."

I chuckled. Once again, Treacle came from around the corner of the house.

"What are you doing, kitty cat?"

"Waiting for you. Had I known you had a police escort…"

"Very funny."

After I pulled out my keys and opened my door, Treacle stood there, supervising, as a parent might two hormonal teenagers.

"Well, thanks for making sure I got home," I said to Blake.

"I'm sorry to hear things with Tom are a little rocky." Blake blurted the words out as if they were watermelon seeds to spit.

"Thanks." I shrugged.

"Do you really think he's *the one?*"

"I never said that," I replied rather quickly. "I don't date very often, so I think my family thought if I liked someone, he must be super-special. I'll try to remember what Jake said about his mom. But." I stepped closer to Blake. "Between you and me, she doesn't like me because I'm just a waitress."

"Some of the most interesting characters in real life wait tables."

"What?" I screwed up my face. "Like who?"

"Frank Capra." Blake put his hands in his pockets and rocked on his heels. "You have seen *It's a Wonderful Life*, haven't you?"

"Of course I have."

He looked at his watch and sighed.

"I've got to get going. This case with Niles Freudenfur is becoming a bigger ball of wax than we expected. Especially since that gunk destroyed our evidence." He rubbed the back of his neck. "We hadn't had a chance to look into the list of names in the date book. It's like the stuff had a timed disintegration mechanism. Just as we were about to take a closer look... poof."

I couldn't help but wonder if that was planned or chance. I didn't say anything. Just shrugged.

"Well, have a good night, Cath. I'll see you tomorrow."

"Good night, Blake."

15

FREE RIDE

"Patrick Fouts showing up at the police station is very odd indeed," my aunt said after we told her what Jake had said. "They said he had a prowler, and he was sure someone was lurking around Niles's property? He didn't see us the other night?"

"No," Bea answered. "He said some slimy-looking thing was lurking around."

"He wasn't at his house when Bea and I tried to call on him," Aunt Astrid said. "I wonder if he's around now."

"It's just a little after eight in the morning." I scratched my head and yawned.

"Maybe he is just getting home at this hour," Bea added. "What do you say we go give it a try?"

"Field trip!" I shouted, clapping and hopping up and down. "I'm driving."

After fifteen minutes, we arrived, and Bea was a little upset.

"What's the rush?" She patted her bright-red curls in place. "You went through so many red lights that I'd be ashamed to tell Jake about it."

"Then don't tell him. And for your information, they were yellow."

"My gosh, you are blind, and you are driving." She shook her head and smoothed her skirt as we walked up to a quaint brownstone.

"He lives here, eh?"

It was a beautiful dark-brown brick building with three floors, the perfect stoop for sitting on, and a garden in the basement, which had an open sliding glass door.

"Let's try there." I pointed.

"We can't just walk in."

"No, but we can yell. He might be in trouble. Yikes, you'd think he'd clean up some of this mud from the plants and stuff." I gingerly went down the cement steps to the door and peeked in. "Hello? Hello? Patrick?"

"Who the hell is it!" The man's voice sounded

anything but threatening, and there was a singsongy accent to his voice.

"Patrick Fouts?" I called again. "You left your door open. Are you all right?"

We heard the pounding of feet on hardwood, but before we saw anyone, the front door on the second floor opened up.

"Oh, hello." A lovely older woman wearing a stylish hat and carrying a briefcase stepped out. "Are you looking for Patrick?" She said it as if young women were always looking for Patrick. Bea and I weren't sure that was accurate, but who were we to say otherwise?

"Um, yes. So sorry to disturb you." Bea spoke kindly and reached out her hand, making quick introductions.

"I'm Laura Fouts, Patrick's mother. I'm sure he'll be out in just a spell. I'm off to work. Have a lovely day, ladies."

And with that, Laura was off down the street to hail a cab.

"Patrick. Can we talk to you for a second?" I stepped closer to the door and caught a glimpse of a tall, thin man putting on a robe. Finally, with as much attitude as we both expected, Patrick came to the sliding door.

The dark circles around his eyes were a stark contrast to his pale complexion and strawberry-blond hair. He reeked of cigarettes and booze. It must have been a late night.

"What?" he barked nervously. "Who are you with? I don't know how many times I have to tell you guys I don't have it."

"Um, no," I blurted out.

Bea was much more diplomatic than me and within seconds managed to get us inside the apartment.

"We wanted to task you about Niles Freudenfur."

His face became even more pained than the hangover he was suffering from made it.

"Are you the police? I've already told you what I know. I wasn't anywhere around when Niles died."

"We aren't with the police," I said. "We just have a few questions."

Bea placed her hand on Patrick's forearm. I was sure in his agitated state, he'd yank it away, but he didn't. Instead, he sank down on the white leather sofa and sighed.

Bea took a seat next to him. I remained standing.

"We heard you were friends with Niles. We just wanted to know if Niles mentioned anything strange that he was working on or maybe experiencing."

Bea's voice was firm but motherly. It was easy to see why people opened up to her. I, on the other hand, got people like Dolores Eversol spilling their guts to me. Loonies.

"Niles mention something strange? If he was talking, you can bet it was something strange. That was how he made his living." Patrick ran his hand through his cropped hair.

"How long did you work for Niles?" Bea continued.

"I didn't work for him. Well, not in the traditional sense."

"What do you mean?" I asked.

"Niles liked to have me around as sort of a prop. Don't get me wrong—I didn't mind. He bought me clothes and paid off half my student loan. He was going to pay for my headshots to get my modeling career going, but then... *this* happened."

"Were you a couple?" I had to ask.

Patrick snickered as if I'd just asked if he'd like to put his hand into a bowl of peeled grapes.

"He wanted to be." Patrick blinked his blue eyes.

"You didn't?" Bea asked gently. Through the course of the exchange, Bea had taken Patrick's hand. She was obviously reading something and trying to coax a little more out of Patrick with a few delicately asked questions.

"You know what Niles looked like. Put him in a dress, and at best, he was Norman Bates's mother... at the end of the movie."

"That's a little harsh," I said, more to myself than really out loud.

"He had a way with some of the women in town. You know, the ones who live in Sarkis Estates and the like. There were some ladies who dropped five K just to sit with Niles for twenty minutes. There were other women who didn't go on a date, accept a job, make a renovation to their home, or send their kid to a certain college if Niles didn't give them the green light."

I rolled my eyes. Aunt Astrid would give them the straight dope for twenty bucks and even throw in an oatmeal raisin cookie for free if your news was a little disappointing.

"This bothered you?" Bea asked.

"No. A fool and his money... you know the rest." Patrick chuckled again. "Besides, a good bit of that money went to me."

"Didn't you feel guilty taking it?" I asked. "Knowing that Niles was a fraud?"

"He wasn't a fraud." Patrick crossed his legs like

a woman and tugged his robe shut. "He may not have had an actual gift of sight. But sometimes you just have to fake it till you make it."

"Is that what you did? Fake it?" I asked. I was getting tired of hearing this spoiled brat talk. He lived in the basement of his mother's brownstone in a posh part of the city. He wanted to be a model because... I doubted there was much more he could do.

"Niles let me in on a lot of his business. I didn't ask for him to bring me into the inner sanctum. But he did." Patrick began to nervously tug at the belt of his robe. "He said he knew of a way we could be together. Forever. He said he just needed to wait until a certain date, and it would all be set. I had no idea what he was talking about. But then..."

"What?" I was not nearly as couth as Bea. I just wanted to know the answers. Forget all this melodrama and spill the beans.

"Niles told me that he'd perform this spell that would unite us forever. He had this crazy look in his eyes like I was a piece of meat or property. I'd never seen it before." Patrick swallowed hard and rubbed his head. "I got scared and told him I wasn't ready for that kind of commitment. You know, the guy was seventy-five. You'd think he'd understand.

But it made him mad. He told me I owed him for all the money he spent on me. What did I think—that it was just a free ride?" Patrick rolled his eyes. "Quite frankly, that is what I thought it was. I thought I'd be out of there with some cash long before he ever demanded anything physical from me."

"So, you were after his money?" Bea had a way of making that sick accusation sound almost cute.

"You would be, too, if he bought you everything you wanted." There wasn't a shred of remorse in Patrick's face as he continued. "But when I saw that he wasn't going to play nice anymore, I threatened to tell his high-rolling clients that he was a fraud. I told him I'd ruin his reputation. Some of those people made life-or-death decisions based on his *seeing the future*. I mean real heavy decisions. Like to get chemotherapy or not, or to get a divorce or not. I couldn't say how many lives he ruined. But let's face it, if you are seeking a psychic to ask whether or not you should get chemo, you are pretty far gone already."

"Niles didn't like that, I'll bet," I said once I pulled my jaw off the floor.

"I told the police I saw him about two weeks before they found his body. He told me that was when the ritual was to start. That was when we had our fight."

"Did you witness any of the ritual?" Bea asked carefully.

"When Niles came at me with one of those squiggly knives you see in all those old sorcerer movies, I left. I haven't been back in the house since."

"Not even once?" I prodded.

How would he be able to tell Jake and Blake there was a person prowling around the grounds if he hadn't come back to the house? He looked up at me and bit his lip.

"I went back once. There has been a prowler around my house. He wears a scary mask that looks like mud or slime or something. I thought..." Patrick's eyes began to water. "I thought that maybe Niles had come back from the dead and was looking to make good on his promise that we'd be together. Forever, like he said."

Bea took both of Patrick's hands in hers.

"You'll be all right, Patrick."

When Bea stood up, she wobbled a little. I slipped my arm through hers and pulled her toward the sliding door, which was still open.

"You might want to remember to close your sliding door," I called over my shoulder.

"I was a little drunk when I got home." He chuckled as we left. I wasn't surprised that was his reply.

"So? What did you get from that?" I asked, helping Bea into the car.

"That man is not going to live much longer if he doesn't change," Bea said as she let out a deep breath.

I handed her a bottle of water that was underneath the front seat. Bea took a long drink and shook her head.

"He's a whirlpool of blackmail and lies and guilt. Not to mention a good deal of vodka and maybe a hint of some kind of narcotic. What a waste."

I got in the car, and we sped back to the café. When we got there, I was shocked to see another scary thing had shown up. Tom and his mother.

❧ 16 ❧

PSYCHIC POWERS

"T his is a nice surprise," I lied as I walked in behind Bea. "What are you guys doing here?"

"We were hoping to have some coffee and a sweet roll or something with you before I had to go off to work, but you weren't here." Tom's voice was aggravated.

"I had something I had to do with Bea this morning. I thought you were bogged down with work and that's why you didn't call." I shot back with a smile. "If I'd known you were coming, I would have adjusted my schedule."

Now, some people said I looked for trouble. I wouldn't say I actively looked for it. I just had the tendency to spot it before it got close. When I looked over at Tom's mother, I could have sworn she was smiling.

Sure, maybe it was an uncomfortable grin for an uncomfortable situation between her son and his girlfriend. But I couldn't help but get the feeling that Patience was enjoying this.

I tried to remember what Jake said. Reaching out an olive branch right now was nearly impossible, but I choked out the words.

"Patience, if you aren't in a hurry, maybe you'd like to stay and have coffee with me." Surprisingly, I sounded convincing. I looked at Tom. "Would that be okay?"

"I think that would be fine," Patience replied, but she came across as though she were making a chess move instead of really accepting my invitation to get to know me.

Tom's feathers smoothed a little.

"Well, I wish I could stay, but I'm already going to be late. I'll call you tonight." He kissed me quickly on the cheek and hurried out of the café.

"Patience, what can I get you?" I smiled as if all I ever wanted was to wait on Patience Warner some-time in my life.

"Just a bottled water," she said.

"Would you like a almond croissant or one of

Bea's peanut-butter bars? Kevin, our baker, also made some oatmeal coo—"

"Just the water."

I nodded and smiled. When I turned around, I caught a glimpse of Aunt Astrid. She'd looked as though she'd just licked a lemon as she studied Patience.

"So what are you going to do today while Tom is at work?" I asked, handing Patience the bottle and taking a seat at one of the tables for two by the window.

"Why don't we not pretend we really want to get to know each other?" She smiled a horrible, condescending grin at me.

"What?" I felt as if I'd been slapped.

"I know all about you. You are all that Tom has talked about for the past couple of months. The waitress at the coffee shop."

She said those words as though they were a disease.

"I'm sure you are very nice. But you and Tom, you're a temporary thing."

"Did he say that?"

"No. You did."

"What?" I shook my head. "I never said any such thing. Even though I'm not reserving a hall in June, I care very much about Tom." I leaned across the table just so I wouldn't have to talk too loudly. "You don't know anything about me."

"I know more than you think." Her right eyebrow arched. "There is someone else who is more complementary to your... lifestyle. Tom won't be on the police force for much longer. When he leaves it, you'll be feeling betrayed and disappointed like he promised you something. You'll resent him. That will be the end."

"Do you really think it's the uniform that does it for me? What do I look like? A teenager? I'm a grown woman, and I know why I feel for Tom the way I do."

As much as I wanted to tell Patience she was wrong, my gut twisted as if it had been suddenly poked. I was afraid she'd hit a nerve.

"Why is that?" Patience smirked. This was her sport.

My eyes began to water. Had I thought I could get away with it, I would have reached across the short span of the table and slapped that look to the floor. But instead I squared my shoulders.

"Because he accepts me for what I am," I nearly whispered.

"And what is that?" It was as if she were feeding

off my sadness. Under her gaze, I wanted to just shrink under the table. Why was this person doing this to me? She was like a middle-aged Darla Castellano, my high school nemesis.

"You know, Cath, I heard that your mother and father left because of you. Is that true?"

With Darla, the deaths of my parents were fair game. If I were to ask her about it now, she probably wouldn't even remember having said that to me. But as a sophomore, she might as well have punched me in the face.

I had the feeling she and Patience would probably get along famously.

"I'm different," I said to Patience. It was the truth. I wasn't going to give her any more ammunition to shoot at me with. "And this is my family's café. The water is on me." I got up and started toward the kitchen.

"Cath, just wait one minute."

She actually said that. As if I was going to continue to sit and listen to her make fun of me. There was no way I was going to say another word to her. Not now, probably not ever.

My thoughts went back to Jake, who had made so much sense last night. I wasn't going to enjoy telling him he was utterly, completely wrong about Tom's mother and he was to never give me advice on meeting parents ever again.

I went into the kitchen just in time for Treacle to slink inside.

"What's wrong?" he asked immediately.

"Tom's mother is out there. She wasn't very nice. I'm just waiting for her to leave."

"There is something wrong with her. I sensed it before."

"You did warn me." The cat slunk over and rubbed against my leg.

Just then, we heard some shouting.

Kevin turned around. Treacle's ears perked up. I held my breath.

"I know exactly what you are!" It was Aunt Astrid. "You are no longer welcome here! Not now! Not ever!"

Quickly, I scooped up Treacle and burst into the dining room. Patience looked as if she'd seen a ghost. Aunt Astrid looked like a wild woman. Her eyes were wide with judgment. Her hair had fallen from the clips in wisps around her face, and she stood as straight as an arrow, pointing at Tom's mother.

"I see you!" was the last thing my aunt said, and it was enough to make Patience turn and stomp out of the café.

There were two other patrons in the room, who looked on in shock. But they remained in their seats as Aunt Astrid apologized for the disturbance and gave them each a complimentary oatmeal cookie. They were the size of hubcaps, so it was a pretty good deal.

"What in the world? I leave the room for a minute, and look what happens!"

I set my cat on an empty table as I watched Patience hurry past the café window, keeping her head down.

"What's gotten into you?"

My aunt sat down at her table but said nothing.

"Bea?"

Bea looked as if she had an idea of what happened, but since it involved her mother, she was going to wait for permission to say something.

I walked over and took a seat across from Aunt Astrid.

"Are you going to spill it, or am I going to have to resort to torture? You know how much I hate torture. So messy." I shivered then smiled helplessly at my aunt.

She had tears in her eyes.

"Cath, I am afraid you may not see Tom anymore after this." She looked down. "I'm sorry. It was not supposed to turn out this way at all. Things were supposed to be so different."

"Okay, well, I didn't think Patience liked me. After my conversation with her, I was right in my assumption. But what were you yelling for? I thought I handled it just fine."

"You did, Cath. You handled that woman with class. I was very proud of you. But she was not playing fair."

"What do you mean?"

My aunt took a deep breath and looked past me out the picture window.

"Tom's mother has a handful of psychic powers."

"Really?"

It made sense. Tom said he had experienced some strange happenings as a kid. A premonition here, a dream that came true there. He had to have gotten it from somewhere, I guessed.

"But she doesn't use it the same way we do." Aunt Astrid's voice was quiet, as if she were telling me not to worry about the thunder as she was putting me to bed. "First of all, she's not nearly as equipped as *we* are. She didn't know that I could see it the second she showed up here. She thought she was being rather slick studying you, looking for chinks in your armor."

"Why would she do that?"

"From all I could gather, she did it because she could."

"It wasn't to protect Tom? Make sure he wasn't being hoodwinked or maybe put in harm's way?"

I looked at Bea. Her head was tilted to the side. She knew I was recalling what Jake had told me the night before. He'd made it sound so simple.

"Perhaps in her mind, she thought it was to protect Tom. I don't know for sure. But she thought she was getting away with something, and I wanted to make sure she knew she wasn't."

"What was she trying to get away with?" I didn't even really want to know, but the words slipped out anyway.

"Breaking you two up."

"But why?" I was angry and upset and confused all at once. "What's so bad about me?"

"Nothing. There is nothing bad about you, Cath," Aunt Astrid practically yelled. "There are people who see in you what they will never be. Patience Warner saw in you something she coveted. I don't know what it is, but I could guess. You didn't stand a chance because she'd made up her mind long before she ever saw you."

I felt rejected. Maybe I hadn't made the best first

impression. Had I tried a little harder and focused on anyone else that wasn't *me,* maybe she would have liked me.

"She's done it before," Bea piped up. "When I shook her hand that first time, there was a layer of deceit so thick I could cut it with a knife. Somehow, Tom didn't follow the career she wanted. He's got a pretty strong aura. I would expect him to be a tough nut to crack. But when it comes to the women he's dated, well, she hasn't approved of any. They all seem to leave, and Tom hasn't put the pieces together yet. He has no idea it's his mother stirring the pot."

I sat there for a second and thought about this. There was part of me that wanted to say *I'll show her* and go find Tom right away and hold him tight and kiss his lips.

But then I wondered about the other women he'd dated. Who was to say *I* was his soul mate? Maybe his mother had chased her off. Maybe he was supposed to be married to someone else, right now, expecting their third baby, and living in a nice house somewhere.

If I went out with Tom now, it would be for spite, to show that woman I was here and I wasn't going anywhere. *Even though I don't love your son...*

Where did that thought come from?

"Aunt Astrid, what should I do?"

"Unlike Patience, I've got to leave you to make your own decisions. Whatever it is, your cousin and I love you."

"I think maybe I should go wash my face and..."

Just then, Jake and Blake came into the café, looking as if they'd both been punched in the gut.

"What's the matter?"

"We just found Patrick Fouts," Jake said. "He's dead."

✣ 17 ✣

ASPHYXIATION

Jake and Blake said that a neighbor had called to say they heard screaming.

"The brownstones in that neighborhood are right on top of each other," Jake said. "The neighbor who called it in said that Patrick was a jerk. He often made a lot of noise since moving back in with his mother about two years ago."

"They also said he'd stumble home drunk and on more than one occasion would be passed out in the courtyard with the door open all night," Blake added.

Quickly, Bea told her husband that we had just come from there and that we'd said hello to his mother and had a talk with Patrick about his relationship with Niles.

"It couldn't have been more than two hours ago." She looked at Jake apologetically.

"Did you see anything strange while you were there?" Blake asked.

"No. Except that he did leave the door open. We yelled inside to wake him up," I added. Without holding back anything, I also added what he told us about his relationship with Niles.

"How did he die?" Aunt Astrid asked.

"A combination of asphyxiation and blood loss," Blake said as he eyeballed some of Kevin's delicious blonde brownies. I got up and put a few in a sack and handed them to him.

"Blood loss?" I asked.

"He was sliced up pretty good before he had about ten pounds of dirt crammed down his throat." Blake took one brownie and devoured it in seconds. I couldn't help but notice that the more gruesome the case, the bigger the appetite.

"So was it the same person who got Niles?"

Aunt Astrid wedged herself behind the counter to get two large paper cups and filled them with coffee for the detectives. She handed one to me, and I carefully added the cream and sugar for Blake. Jake drank his black.

I also grabbed two veggie subs that were new on

the menu and put those in another sack. The guys were going to need to keep up their strength with this one.

I handed that to Blake too.

"For lunch," I said.

He winked as Jake continued talking. I felt a skip in my chest but ignored it and went to pet Treacle, who had come to say hello to Blake.

Bea leaned over the counter to hold Jake's hands.

"We are pretty sure it's the same person. A very distinctive knife made the wounds on the body. If we found the knife, we'd find the killer. But what would really help is if the murderer just waltzed into the station and turned themselves in," Jake joked.

"If you ladies spoke to Patrick, you'll need to come to the station," Blake said after washing down his second brownie with a sip of hot coffee.

"Of course."

Bea hurried around the counter, squeezing past her mother, to grab her purse, then rushed up to Jake and slipped her hand in his. I sort of moseyed. It had been a really lousy morning, and this was just the cherry on top.

"We'll call you if we need bail money," I said.

I HAD FINISHED ANSWERING QUESTIONS first. We weren't as unlucky as I'd thought since the neighbor who called the police had mentioned seeing two women leave Patrick's place just a short while before all the screaming started.

Since that witness said that the redhead looked a little woozy, Jake was in a dither, fussing over Bea as if they'd reported she had been bleeding from her eyeballs and her lower intestines had fallen out.

"It's been a long morning," I told Blake. "Can you tell Bea I'm heading home?"

"Sure," he mumbled, barely looking up at me. "Do you want me to call your aunt too?"

"That would be nice. Thanks."

"No problem, Cath."

He had been scribbling something that only he could read in a file before he quickly shut it, jumped up from his desk, and stomped to the office at the end of the bullpen, where Bea and I had waited when we first got there.

I looked around. No one even noticed me. So I slung my purse over my shoulder and walked out of the station.

It wasn't a long walk back to the café or home. I was a little worried about the heavens opening up, as the sky was gray. But I managed to make it. I was exhausted, and this wasn't like me. Maybe I was coming down with a cold or something. But it felt as if ten days of drama had been crammed into the past few hours.

Between Tom's mom, Patrick Fouts, and this whole murder case, I couldn't tell what to focus on first. The fact that focusing on Tom wasn't at the forefront of my mind was another issue to cause me angst.

"What is wrong with you, Cath?"

18

AURA WRAP

I decided to do a cleansing. I filled my house with the sweet smell of burning sage and just wallowed in it. Then I did something I hadn't done in years. There were short, simple spells for witches to perform on themselves that acted like exercise did on regular people. I needed to get out of my rut.

In my closet, behind a stack of sweatshirts and a beautiful hatbox filled with keepsakes, was my own spell book. Certainly it was nothing like the library at Aunt Astrid's place. But it was mine.

During the past couple of years, I had collected a spell here, a chant there, and organized them in my little notebook—complete with stickers and happy doodles.

"So let's see," I mumbled. "Psychic alignment? Maybe a hydrating aura wrap? Aromatherapy for a depressed animus. That might work. No. Here's the ticket."

The next page was marked with hearts and smiley faces.

"An invigorating pneuma wash with an aura peel and psychic muscle polishing. Why didn't I think of this sooner?"

This was such a simple procedure that while I collected my supplies—two white candles, a handful of pink crystals, a cotton hankie, and a needle with red thread—I pondered my situation.

"She didn't even give me a chance," I said as I threaded the needle. That was what was really upsetting.

I lit the candles and recited the words I had carefully written down. The crystals were placed in the proper places around me, and then I blew the candles out.

Within minutes, I began to feel the soothing effects of my at-home spa treatment. It helped. After an hour, I felt as if I needed a nap and lay down.

I knew it was later in the day when Treacle hopped up on the bed. I'd gotten into the habit of leaving the window cracked enough for him to come and go as he pleased.

"You've had a rough day?" he asked, head-butting me and purring softly.

"I feel better now," I said as I wrapped him up in my arms.

We both fell back to sleep. When I woke up, it was dusk. I felt like a brand-new person when I reached for the phone and called my aunt.

"No, honey. You just stay home and relax. It'll do you some good. Bea and I can handle it. But…"

"But what?"

"Well, Tom stopped by, looking for you."

"I'll bet he did."

"I'm not sure what his mother told him, but he looked like he really wanted to talk to you."

"Was he mad?"

"No." My aunt sighed. "But he was concerned."

"Okay. I'll take it from here. Thanks, Aunt Astrid."

When I hung up, I had no idea why I had said that. I had no desire to talk to Tom about his mother or anything else. What had happened? Just two weeks ago I had been giddy and giggly over the man. Now, well, I wasn't.

I looked at the clock on my nightstand. I had had

a good rest, but now I was ready to attack the world. I wanted to show off my glowing aura and my finely toned psyche. But as per usual, I was going left when the world was going right.

"Hey, Treacle. You up for an adventure?"

"What do you have in mind?"

"I'm thinking maybe I'd like to take another trip to Niles's house. You in?"

"Why do you want to go back there?"

"I don't know. Because I don't want to just sit around, yet I don't want to talk to anyone. Not anyone who walks on two legs, that is."

"Yeah. I'm in."

I got dressed in dark clothes that covered my arms and legs, even though it was a warm night. The idea of walking on the Freudenfur property gave me images of swarming mosquitos and chiggers.

Before long, we were in the car and just around the corner from Niles's house. This time, there was no party or long line of cars for me to camouflage my car behind.

"I'm going to park a couple blocks away. We'll have to walk."

"Are you sure you want to do this?"

"Why? Are you picking up on something?"

"Not yet. But just give it some time."

I parked on a quiet street around the block where a few other vehicles were parked. Treacle hopped out and sniffed the air, and we began our stroll. It didn't take but a few minutes for both of us to feel a shift in the air.

"*What is that smell?*" I asked as we neared the house.

"*I don't know.*"

"*It's like an old, earthy smell, like a dead tree or stagnant water or something.*"

We kept walking until we were finally at the front of the house.

"*How about it?*" I asked.

Part of me was hoping Treacle might chicken out, and I thought he was hoping I would do the same.

"*Sure. Why not? What could happen at the front of the house?*"

I looked up and down the street. We were the only ones out. As I scanned the houses for any neighbors who might be keeping an eye on the place, I wondered if maybe this was too much. Sure, I was wide-awake after my home-spa day, but I could always watch some television or draw some pictures or do the laundry. Why in the world wasn't I at home, doing the laundry?

Treacle and I slowly walked up the driveway. The

house sat in complete darkness, looking at us as if we were tiny, intrusive ants that could easily be squashed.

Squinting, I looked in the windows. The curtains were closed on all of them except one. Was that the creepy doll room? I tried to match the interior layout to the windows, but I couldn't be sure.

"Stop thinking about those dolls."

Treacle heard me think to myself. *"What dolls?"*

I explained the doll room if for no other reason than to hear myself talk.

There was no porch light. The crescent moon didn't illuminate our path that much. As we got closer, I was sure I could hear something rustling in the trees that flanked the house. There were large hedges of fragrant lilac along the face of the house.

"It's spooky out here, but I'm not picking up anything really weird. Are you?" I asked Treacle. *"And I just did a whole beauty routine on my aura so I'm free of any real blockage. I don't think Bea could have done any better."*

"I'm happy you cleared out your blockage."

"Well, when you put it like that, you make it sound gross."

"I'm especially glad Bea didn't have to do it. I'm sure she is too."

"Very funny, cat."

We crept closer.

"Do you want to go in the house?" Treacle asked.

"I thought we'd just look around the grounds. I don't know what I expected to find. I just thought that maybe…"

Suddenly Treacle stopped. His back began to arch, and I watched in the pale light as his hair stood on end, making him appear at least two sizes bigger than he was.

"Cath."

"Yeah?"

"What's that?"

"What's what?"

Treacle stared at the carport attached to the left side of the house.

"It's just a shadow, right?" I squinted harder. My eyes were drawn up to the window that I thought had no curtain. Strangely, it now appeared to have a curtain over it. Was it a trick of the light or lack thereof? Did I just think the window had no curtain because of the angle from which I was looking at it? Or did someone put the curtain back in place as they saw us approaching?

"That's just a shadow. It's the shadow of one of those lilac bushes," I replied, looking at the hulking wild thing that was at the end of the driveway.

"But it's on the driveway. Niles Freudenfur didn't have

some kind of bush growing out of the middle of his driveway. And it doesn't really look shrubby. It looks sort of humanoid."

I thought back to when we came for the estate sale. No. There was no shrub in the middle of the driveway. What was in the middle of the driveway did not look shrubby. Treacle was right.

"Did you really just say humanoid?"

"It looks like it's dirty. Really dirty. Muddy."

"A dirty, muddy humanoid?"

That was when the thing's eyes opened.

"Shrubs don't have eyes. I've prowled through enough to know." Treacle began to growl.

"Do you see that? Are they red?"

"They look red." He hissed.

"Those aren't lights coming from behind it?"

"No, Cath. Whatever it is, it's a solid thing. It's not a shrub."

"It would be better if it was a shrub."

"But it's not a shrub or a hedge or a plant."

"Are you sure?"

"No. But you are more than welcome to creep a little closer and take a better look. I'll hang back here and—"

The sound pushed into our ears like a man kicking in a door. It was a horrible, guttural scream of hatred, and it was directed at us. The smell of decay and dirt became overwhelming. Still the thing stood there, staring at Treacle and me. We felt those red eyes boring into us.

"I think we'd better go."

"I think we'd better run!"

The creature took two lumbering steps and had closed the distance between us. Treacle, who was naturally faster than I was, darted off like a bullet in the direction we'd come from.

"Meet me at the car!" I yelled before turning and dashing off down the driveway.

I heard the thing scream again and wondered why no one else in any of the surrounding houses came to investigate.

It was an unholy sound that stayed in my ears. As my feet pounded against the driveway, I was sure the thing was right behind me. The smell was overwhelming. My eyes were starting to water. The hairs on the back of my neck were bristling. As I gulped air, my mouth became dryer and dryer as I pushed myself to run even faster. Still, I knew it was gaining on me. It was huge. One of its steps was at least two of mine.

"Hurry, Cath!"

Treacle was perched on top of my car. His back wasn't arched, but his green eyes glinted in the darkness. Those were lovely eyes. Those eyes were comforting and welcoming and familiar. They didn't burn with hatred and strike terror into a person.

"Hurry!"

Struggling not to slow down, I reached into my front pocket for my keys. I pulled the inside of my pocket out as I yanked them free. Thankfully I knew no one would ever want to steal my Dodge Neon, so the door was unlocked.

As my body crashed into the side of the car, I fumbled for the handle. With the kind of precision that only came by being so closely connected, as soon as I yanked open the door, Treacle jumped inside. I threw myself behind the wheel, yanked the door shut, jammed the keys in the ignition, and didn't stick around to see how close the thing had come to my car.

"Thank goodness Bea isn't driving," Treacle said.

I started to laugh with relief.

"Are we going to tell the others?" He stood up on the passenger seat and turned his head to see out the back window.

"I think we should just go home."

Treacle and I didn't say anything else, but he purred next to me the rest of the way home. Once we got there, we quickly and quietly hurried to the front door, and I turned on all the inside lights, slipped the dead bolt, chain, and doorknob locks into place, and double-checked the windows before letting out a breath.

"Sorry, kitty. I'm closing the window for tonight." I locked the sliding kitchen window. "How about a little milk before bed?"

"*I'm not tired.*"

"Me neither. But you can have some milk, anyway."

I snapped the television on and stumbled on *The Best Years of Our Lives*.

"This is a good one," I told Treacle, who hopped up on my bed and curled up on the pillows. "It's about these men coming home after the war. One guy has no hands and has to use his hooks. It's amazing. He could really do all this stuff in real life."

"*That sounds sad.*"

"I think it's inspiring. Plus, this movie is about three hours long. Since I won't be sleeping tonight, at least I won't have to flip through the stations."

Under my bed were a couple of sketchbooks and some fancy drawing pencils. I had been quite the artist in high school. But as grown-up life replaced teenage angst, I found not only did I have less time to draw, but I also had less need to express myself this way. But I had always enjoyed sketching and doodling.

Since tonight was a special situation, I decided to draw what Treacle and I had seen. Over the course of the movie, I sketched and erased and embellished on the page until Treacle approved.

"That's what I saw."

"That's what I saw too." I sighed as I looked at the image of the creature we'd seen. *"Aunt Astrid is going to be mad that we went out there by ourselves."*

"Probably." Treacle yawned. *"But you got a look at it. Maybe she'll recognize it from one of her books."*

"I'll tell her that. It might soften the lecture I'm going to get tomorrow."

Aunt Astrid was forever telling me not to go off on my own when we were dealing with possibly hostile paranormal entities. I really tried to listen to her. It was just that sometimes a person needed a brush with death to feel as if they were really living.

Okay, that wasn't true.

Somewhere, someone who was selfish and maybe a bit crazy said they needed to face death in order to feel alive. That wasn't me. I was just a terrible listener. Plain and simple.

❧ 19 ❧

A SPELL ON YOU

"What is all over the back of your car?" Bea pointed as she crossed the street the next morning.

"What?" I asked.

"Did someone vandalize your car?"

"They'd better not have!" I trotted out the front door to take a look at what she was pointing at.

What I saw made my blood run cold.

"What jerk would put muddy handprints on your car?" She leaned forward with her eyes narrowed. "At least, I hope that's mud."

"It's mud," I mumbled. I slung my purse with my sketchbook in it over my shoulder and slipped my arm through Bea's. "Let's get to the café."

"What's the matter with you? You're shaking."

"I'd rather just spill it all at once than have to repeat myself."

Bea nodded and patted my hand as we hurried to the café.

"CATH, WHAT AM I SUPPOSED TO DO WITH you?" Aunt Astrid scolded. "When are you ever going to learn that we are stronger together? When one of us goes off to wade in a pool of danger, it can be harmful to us all!"

"I'm sorry, Aunt Astrid. I was feeling restless last night, and I had Treacle with me. I wasn't totally alone. His magic helped."

"What would you do if something happened to him? If your cousin and I and the other cats weren't there to help him? What would you do if you were overwhelmed and Treacle was left alone?"

"I don't know what to say except I'm sorry."

My aunt waddled to the door in her usual way of maneuvering through the dimensions she could see and flipped the sign on the door to read Open. Within minutes, a steady flow of customers, familiar and new, came to get their morning jolt of coffee or tea or flourless chocolate cake.

I didn't speak to anyone unless spoken to, and Bea, as usual, handled all the friendly chatter. It wasn't clear if Aunt Astrid was ignoring me or letting me do my job uninterrupted. She barely looked at me and hardly said a word.

I felt terrible.

Finally, there was a lull in foot traffic. I took a seat at the counter across from Bea. I ordered myself a mint tea and a slice of carrot cake. The cake was so moist that had it been stirred just one more time, it might have become pudding.

"Have you tasted this?" I asked Bea.

She shook her head, so I sliced off a wedge and let her have it.

"Holy moly." She rolled her eyes. "That is so good."

"What does Kevin do to get the texture and the frosting so perfect that..."

"Cath," Aunt Astrid interrupted.

"Yes?" I replied quickly, eager to do anything my aunt wanted if it meant her forgiving me for being so reckless.

"Are you going to hoard all that cake, or do I get a bite too?"

I smiled.

I got up from my seat, walked around the counter, got Aunt Astrid her own slice, and dropped the money in the till. We got almost everything to eat for free. But I hoped she would understand my gesture and forgive me quickly. There was still so much more to tell her.

"Cath, you are a grown woman. I can't tell you what to do. If your mother were still here, I'll bet she would have been knocking on your door, inviting you to do exactly what you did last night. You are so much alike. I forget sometimes that you are not my real daughter. You have her looks, her mannerisms, her stubbornness." She winked when she said that. "But I've told you before, and I'll tell you again. I love you like you were my own daughter. And that means I will slap you silly if you think you can get away with going off ghost hunting by yourself in the middle of the night."

"I'm sorry, Aunt Astrid," I answered. "From now on, the buddy system or nothing."

"Good girl. Wow." She said after taking a bite of the cake. "What are we charging for this?"

"A dollar seventy-five a slice," Bea answered.

"Knock it up to two dollars. This is too good. People will pay." She dabbed the corners of her mouth with a napkin then squinted at me. "For your punishment, young lady, you are not allowed to eat any more of Kevin's carrot cake."

"For how long?" I griped. This was getting out of hand. I was willing to sit in the corner until Aunt Astrid cooled off, but depriving me of Kevin's carrot cake was cruel and unusual punishment.

"Until you learn your lesson. And rest assured it will be on the menu for the next couple of weeks. Just to drive the point home."

My aunt took another bite and arched her eyebrows. I was beaten.

So now that the scolding was over, I told my aunt I had more to tell her. When I pulled out my sketchbook and showed her my rendition of the creature that chased Treacle and me, she swallowed hard.

"So I was right," she muttered. "Niles tried *The Sequence of Ursaken*, botched it up, and released this abomination."

"You know what it is?" I asked.

"This is a revenge demon."

"Demon? Did you say demon?" Bea stuttered.

"I did." She stared at the image as if she were half expecting it to jump off the page and start tearing apart the café. With trembling hands, she closed my sketchbook and handed it back to me.

"We have to get rid of this thing. It isn't like anything we've ever dealt with before." She looked into my eyes. "You said it saw you?"

"Yes." I already didn't like the sound of that.

"That's probably the gunk that is on the back of your car, Cath," Bea added, making my aunt's eyes widen.

"What's on your car?"

"When Treacle and I ran out of there, we hopped in the car and drove away. But this morning, there were two muddy handprints on my car."

Aunt Astrid pinched her lips together.

"We've got to move quickly," Aunt Astrid said. "You ladies stay here. It's business as usual as far as you are concerned. I'm going back to my house. I'm going to do some research to make sure this is indeed the creature I think it is. If so, the preparation needed to get ready for this will take me a couple of hours."

"Shouldn't we stick together?" Bea asked. "You're always saying how much stronger we are together. And if we are dealing with a demon this time, maybe separating isn't the best route to take."

"While the sun is up, we're fine. This creature, like those of its kind, doesn't like the sun. It prefers shadows and darkness." My aunt's usually jovial expression had transformed into a tombstone of seriousness. "Tonight, I suggest we all stay together. That includes Jake and Blake."

"Blake? Why does he need to be with us?" I asked a little too quickly.

"Because he might be in danger too. He and Jake were both on the scene at Niles's house."

"But they didn't see the creature," I replied nervously. For some reason, the idea of having Blake wrapped up in this made me jittery inside.

My aunt looked at me with a twinkle in her eyes. It was as if she was reading something much deeper in my expression. I felt my cheeks get red.

"It's going to be all right, Cath," she assured me. "It's going to be fine. Now, you two continue along as I said. If I need you to bring me anything, I'll call. Otherwise, get ahold of Jake and tell him he and Blake are to come over for dinner."

Bea nodded, and I shifted from one foot to the other.

A few hours went by with just enough business traipsing through the café to keep Bea and me from really talking.

The lunch-hour rush was slow but steady.

The after-dinner hour had a dozen people meandering in and out of the place at an excruciatingly slow pace.

Finally, around six o'clock, we got a lull.

"What did I do?" I asked Bea after the day was almost over. "I really stepped in it, didn't I?"

"Why did you go to the house?" Bea asked.

I told her about my special spa night and how much better I had felt and that I couldn't sleep.

"You can always call me if you can't sleep, Cath." Bea smiled and patted my shoulder.

"I wanted to make a decision about Tom."

"Are you two having trouble? Aside from with the mother, I mean." Bea blinked her wide eyes.

"Ever since I met her, there has been a shift in the air. I know what Aunt Astrid said and that it isn't me. But how do you go back to the way things were when you know that she's scheming behind your back?" I clicked my tongue. "The really sad thing about it is that I'm not sure I even care anymore. How did this happen? How did I wake up one day and feel... 'Tom? Meh.'" I shrugged.

"We can't control how we feel abut someone any more than we can control the stars in the sky," Bea said.

"But a month ago, I didn't feel like this."

"A month ago, you hadn't met his mother."

"Do you think she put a spell on me?" I asked, getting madder by the second.

"No. Her trying to inflict a spell on you would be as effective as shooting a spitball at you. She's obviously not a real witch. You also just had what sounded like a wonderful evening pampering yourself. All that would have removed any whammy she might have tried to put on you." Bea poured a coffee for one of our regular customers, who chatted on his cell phone as he did every evening on his way home.

"So what I'm feeling, or not feeling, is all me."

"Looks that way," Bea said.

Just as I was about to rant some more, Jake and Blake walked in. My heart fluttered as if I were coming straight down the steep end of a roller-coaster. I accidentally jiggled a couple cups, almost knocking them to the floor.

"Hi, honey," Bea said, leaning over the counter for a kiss from Jake.

He was always happy to oblige. Blake took a seat in front of me as I rolled my eyes at the pair.

"Coffee?" I asked with a smirk.

"Yes. Hold the sugar. Jake and Bea are sweet enough," he replied without so much as cracking a grin. I, on the other hand, laughed out loud.

"Will this be to go?"

"No. For here. We've got some time to kill," Blake said.

"Oh yeah? How come?" I asked.

"The murder of Niles Freudenfur was enough, but now we've got Patrick Fouts killed in the same way, and he has a mother who is beyond hysterical, demanding we do something. As if we are sitting on a suspect, waiting for the right time to pull him out of a sack." Jake harrumphed as he took a seat on the stool next to Blake.

Just as I was about to help Bea get the coffee for the boys, the phone rang.

"Brew-Ha-Ha Café," I answered.

"Cath?" It was Tom. I coughed and felt my stomach fall into my shoes. What was wrong with me? Shouldn't I be happy to hear from him?

"Hi, Tom. What's up?" I turned around so that no one in the café could see my face or hear my conversation. Not that it was much of a conversation. I had no idea what to say.

"Are you going to be around tonight?"

"Yeah." I thought lazily. "I'm here until closing at seven thirty. Why?"

"I think we need to talk. My mom told me what happened and…"

"It's okay, Tom. We don't need to talk about that." I grimaced at the idea of discussing what Patience had said and how my aunt stepped in. It was embarrassing. Not for me. I didn't do anything. It was embarrassing for Tom to have to come and make excuses for his witchy-wannabe mom.

"We do. Can I stop by tonight? Before closing?"

"Sure." I tried to sound as if I were excited, but it came off phony. "I'll be here."

"Good. Okay. See you tonight, Cath."

Before I could stop myself, I just hung up the phone. I didn't say good-bye or see ya or kiss my butt.

"Classy, Cath," I muttered.

"Who was that?" Bea asked.

"Nobody," I skulked and looked at Blake, who was diligently reading his notes as Jake talked to Bea about the case.

The guys stayed for a little while. Each had a slice of Kevin's sinfully good carrot cake for dessert.

I scoffed at Blake. "I hope you enjoy that carrot cake."

"Don't you like it?"

"It is the best thing I've ever tasted. But I sort of promised my aunt I wouldn't eat any of it." I didn't say anything more. I didn't want to explain to Blake that I was being punished like a teenager who snuck out her window the night before and got caught.

"In that case, I'll take two slices to go."

I looked Blake square in the eyes. He didn't flinch.

"You are a piece of work," I grumbled. I said good-bye to two slices and snapped them in a container. Then, with a pinch more bad attitude, I handed them over. "Enjoy."

As I was staring daggers at Blake, Jake got a call on his cell. He stepped outside to take it, leaving Blake staring at me as if I were some kind of fungus culture under a microscope.

Jake came back into the café, shaking his head.

"What's wrong?"

"A witness on another case is getting cold feet about testifying in court tomorrow." Jake tugged at the collar of his shirt. "He's a bit needy. I think this is more for show, but the captain wants me to bring him to the station and give him a good talking-to."

"You need me on this?" Blake asked.

"No."

Blake nodded and went back to his notes.

"I'll see you at home?" Jake said to Bea as he took her hand in his and brought it to his lips for a kiss.

"Mom wants us for dinner at her house." Bea giggled.

"Fine by me. I'll meet you at her house." Jake clapped Blake on the back, promising to call him later.

When Jake left, so did the remaining customers. The foot traffic slowed to a crawl.

"Can you leave the café for a spell?" Blake asked out of nowhere.

I looked at the clock. It was six thirty. "Yeah. Why?"

"I've got a couple errands to run and could use your help."

I looked at him suspiciously.

"You are asking for my help? You wouldn't ask me for help on how to spell my own name. What's up?"

"Why are you so suspicious? There are dozens of scientific papers that say paranoia goes hand in hand with several other mental disorders. A literal mind over matter revised way of thinking could correct the psychosis and add years onto your life."

"Me, suspicious?" I tilted my head like a dog that heard a high-pitched whine.

"Grab your purse," he said as he stood up. "Bea,

I'm borrowing your cousin for a minute. I'll bring her back shortly."

"Are you all right being by yourself?" I asked.

"I'm going to lock it up a little early, so don't worry. Just go straight to Mom's when you guys are done." Bea began wiping down the counter and emptying the coffeepots.

I kissed Bea on the cheek, grabbed my purse, and followed Blake to his car.

"So where are we going?"

"Niles Freudenfur's place."

I stopped in my tracks.

Blake turned around and looked at me. "What's wrong?"

"Why do you want to go there?"

"We've gotten a couple calls about a prowler. Some strange noises too. I didn't pay too much attention to Patrick Fouts when he said he saw a prowler around there. I thought he was a grubby gold-digger looking to take advantage of an old has-been. Now he's dead. I should have listened to my gut."

"What does your gut tell you now?"

"That there is something strange about that house."

"Why do you need me?"

"I don't. I just thought it would be a safe place for you to eat this carrot cake."

He jiggled the bag in the air, still without a smile or even a smirk, and then continued walking to his car.

I shook my head and hurried after him.

20

AS VALUABLE AS VACCINES

By the time I finished the second slice of carrot cake, I was completely immersed in the surveillance we were conducting on the Freudenfur house.

"So how are things with you and Tom?" Blake asked.

Up until this point the conversation had revolved around clues and evidence and some people who were interviewed. Blake had a few things to say about Dolores Eversol like *prone to exaggerate* and *in need of some old-fashioned manners*. But when he asked me about Tom, things suddenly shifted.

"I don't know." I sighed.

"What do you mean, you 'don't know'?"

Without going into the witchy details, I told him

about the first and second encounter with his mother.

"Truthfully, Blake, something is just missing. That might sound stupid, but it's the best way I can describe it."

"I know how you feel. That was how I felt about Darla."

The carrot cake that had tasted so good going down was now burning the back of my throat as I controlled the urge to vomit.

"The chemical reactions that go on between people are as valuable as vaccines are in preventing negative outcomes." He meticulously explained something about pheromones and physiological experiments and studies that proved certain body types went with other body types, and it felt as if I were back in school, getting a lecture by a good-looking yet terribly dry professor.

"What about love?" I interrupted. "Science doesn't explain why we love who we love. And I was raised that when you find *The One*, you know it. I don't think there are any reports or studies that explain that."

"So you are one of those hopeless romantic types? Is that what you're saying?" Blake looked through a small set of binoculars in the direction of Niles's house.

"Yeah. So?"

"Nothing. I'm not surprised."

There it was. There was the condescending tone that could only come from Blake Samberg.

"What is that supposed to mean?" I snapped. "If you had it all figured out with your formulas and equations, you would have seen that Darla was not only not the one but so far in the opposite direction you should have fallen off the map."

Blake didn't flinch but kept looking at the house. Since I didn't get his immediate attention, I continued lecturing him.

"I'm not a descendant of Spock's, okay? I have emotions and feelings, and I'm not afraid to let them guide me. It's not always logical. I'm not a Romulan. I'm a human."

"Vulcan."

"What?"

"Spock was a Vulcan. Actually, he was half-Vulcan, half-human. His father married a human woman."

"I'm going to punch you in the face," I retorted.

"Then I'll have to arrest you for assaulting an officer."

Before I could say another word, he pointed toward the house. From our vantage point, we could see a sliver of the front yard. But it seemed that Blake was more interested in what was happening in the backyard. That only made sense since no one in their right mind would go traipsing up the driveway… like me.

We were looking at the area Aunt Astrid, Bea, and I had traveled when we trespassed on the property. When we heard that terrible screeching and bolted out of there.

"I think I see movement." He put the binoculars down. "Stay close, and don't make any noise."

"What? Are you crazy? We can't go on the property."

"Why not? The owner is dead. No one else should be on the premises."

"That includes us, right?"

"My badge gives us dispensation."

Blake opened the door and climbed out of the car. I quickly followed him but wondered why I didn't just stay put. Aunt Astrid was really going to kill me, if the creature I saw last night didn't first.

"Blake!" I hissed. "Blake! Wait!"

He turned around and stopped just as we reached the edge of the property. It was the same as when

Aunt Astrid, Bea, and I had attempted to snoop around. Should I tell Blake we'd been here? That there was a hidden altar that was overgrown with the wrong kind of pentagram painted on it? Maybe I should tell him I was here last night, that this was my third visit to the Freudenfur estate, and none of them ended in any other way than me running away from some screaming, lumbering thing that had gotten so close to me yesterday that it tagged my car with its muddy, grubby hands.

"What?" he asked quietly, pulling me down into the tall grass to stay out of sight.

"I have to tell you something. I was here last night," I confessed. "I saw something. I don't know how to tell you what it was. But it was bad, and I really think we should go back to my aunt's house."

"What did you see?"

I couldn't tell him. If it were Tom, I could. I could say that I saw a man who looked as if he was made of mud and slime and smelled like a swamp. But I couldn't tell Blake. The words wanted to come out, but they just wouldn't.

"I... can't be sure."

"Someone is doing something inside that house. They are looking for something that was left behind or hidden that will help solve this case. I've got to find them and see what they are trying to hide."

Maybe Blake was right. That made a lot more sense than some sludge creature, that was for sure. Maybe, since Niles was a warlock, in the loosest of terms, someone thought a spooky story would keep people away. Maybe I was wrong all along and it wasn't the demon Aunt Astrid said it was. Maybe it was just some guy in a mask.

"Come on." Blake took my hand. We locked our fingers to make sure we weren't letting go. It felt as if we'd been holding hands like this our whole lives. I didn't feel the butterflies or jitters as I had with Tom. Instead, I felt brave.

We inched our way closer to the house, but there was nothing moving around. In fact, it was as still as a graveyard. A few crickets chirped quickly. I listened for any other footsteps but heard nothing.

By the time I realized my hand was sweating, Blake and I were near the overgrown pond at the edge of the back porch. The sky was clear, but the moon had not risen yet. We were in the darkest dark I'd ever seen. I could feel my pupils trying to stretch even wider to grasp any extra shard of light that might help things come into focus.

Without thinking, I leaned closer to Blake.

With his free hand, he reached into his jacket. I was afraid he was pulling out his gun. What was he going to shoot at? Unless he had eyes like Treacle he'd just be aiming into the darkness. A blind man had a better chance of hitting a target.

Blake leaned so close to my ear to speak to me his lips were almost touching my skin.

"Do you hear that?"

I held my breath and listened.

There was a sucking sound. It was that soggy, wet sound a boot made when being pulling out of mud.

I turned my head toward him and could feel his cheek so close to me as he leaned close to listen.

"Yes."

We stood motionless with our hands still locked when I felt more than saw Blake extend his arm. There was a click and then a shadow-shattering beam of light. His flashlight lit up half the backyard.

He'd aimed it to his right. I wasn't sure what Blake was expecting to find. If he thought there was a person trespassing or vandals looking to break into the old house, I could have warned him he'd be disappointed. But what he saw, what *we* saw, changed everything.

21

GROWLS AND GURGLES

At first, it looked as though some kind of muddy substance was spilling out of the pond. It rolled over itself like lava from a volcano. But before Blake could say anything, an arm shot out of the muck, followed by the second. They pulled from the ooze a torso that arched, ultimately throwing back what could only be the head.

That horrible, hateful scream came from the open maw.

"Cath? Am I hallucinating?"

"No! No, Blake!" I wasn't sure what state Blake's mind was in. But I wasn't going to leave him here. When I turned around to face the house, there was a mist swirling around the corners. There was no way

I was going to run, pulling Blake into that. "Come on!"

We both turned and ran to the back door. I remembered from the estate sale that the back door had been barricaded. Before I could say we'd have to break a window Blake kicked it open and pulled me inside.

The fog was all around the house. We could see it through the thin curtains left hanging across the front windows.

"What is that?"

"I don't know!" I panted. "Come on!"

I was sure I could hear the sloshy, thick steps of the mud creature closing in on us. It was making its way up the back porch.

"Upstairs!"

The bright light lit everything up for us, but it also alerted the thing to where we were headed. I pulled Blake down the hallway to what had been the doll room. Thankfully, it was empty of the glassy-eyed devils that had been there just a few days earlier.

"In here," I whispered as I pulled him toward the closet.

"How do you know about this?"

"Get in, and I'll tell you everything," I hissed as I

yanked open the second tiny door inside the closet with the crystal doorknob.

Blake pulled the big closet door shut behind him then shined the light into the smaller opening. The room was so small we had to crouch to get in. The ceiling was slanted. The floor was unfinished. The walls were skeletal beams alternating with pink fiberglass.

Quickly but quietly, I pulled the small door shut. We both held our breath and listened. The thing was screaming again. Was it in the house? Was it looking for us outside in that strange fog?

Blake had to kneel down. He was too tall for the small room. I was stooping when I realized we were still holding hands. We'd let go when we got to the closet. But our hands had automatically found each other again.

"Get behind me," he whispered.

We could both hear the thing pounding slowly up the steps.

"No. You get behind me." I gently pushed him back.

"Cath, I don't know what that thing was, but it looked like a man. You're just too small. If I have to use my gun, I want you behind me."

"Your gun won't work. But do you have any silver on you?"

"What?"

"I don't have time to explain. Do you?"

Blake reached inside his shirt and pulled out a silver chain.

"Can I have it?"

He yanked hard and broke the clasp to a small St. Jude medal. I knew St. Jude was the patron saint of police officers and lost causes. Tom had one too. *How appropriate,* I thought. Blake was a cop, but I wondered if he wasn't more of a lost cause. The thought made me chuckle inside, but I didn't say anything.

"Give me your pencil," I ordered quietly.

Without asking, he gave me his pencil. Without worrying about what he was going to think of me, I drew a quick circle on the floor. Reciting a couple of lines from a childhood protection spell I'd learned from my mother, I touched the silver charm to the sides of the circle. I did the same kind of thing to the little door, hoping it would be enough to keep us safe until either the thing gave up or the sun came up. Whichever came first.

I gently took Blake's hand again. He didn't pull away from me. In fact, I felt his hand tighten around mine. We sat down in the circle. It wasn't a big space. We had to almost snuggle together.

"I always knew there was something about you," Blake said, barely over a whisper. He didn't let go of my hand.

"What do you mean?" I said, more in an effort to distract myself from the horror that I was sure was climbing up the steps, ready to sniff us out.

"You have a gift, don't you?"

"That's one way to put it."

He let go of my hand. I pretended not to be hurt.

"Does it bother you?" I prodded.

"I've just seen a man crawl out from a muddy, disgusting pond and take off after us. There are bigger things bothering me right now than you."

I chuckled.

We heard the thing outside. Both of us froze.

"Light," I whispered, pointing to the flashlight.

Blake clicked off the light. We were immersed in an even blacker black than we had been in outside. I waved my hand in front of my face. I couldn't see a thing.

"This is my hand," Blake said as he slipped his arm around my shoulder. "Don't be scared, Cath."

"I'll try."

"Whatever you did with my medal, it'll work."

"I hope you're right."

The thing continued to shuffle along the hallway, screaming in frustration and stomping every couple of feet as if it thought to run but changed its mind.

We heard it getting closer.

I started to tremble. I couldn't help it. Blake tightened his arm around me, pulling me into him as he positioned himself between the door and me.

Now, some people might say it was the wrong time to notice how strong Blake's arms were beneath his old suit and that even though we were both sweating in the tiny room as much from fear as from the temperature, he still smelled good.

What was I doing? I was distracted. I needed to concentrate on the spell to keep us safe. I might as well have taken Blake's pencil and made little hearts and curlicues for all the good this protection circle was going to do us.

"It's in the room," Blake whispered in my ear.

We froze and listened.

The sounds that came from this creature were like many growls and gurgles by a symphony of wild animals.

It knew where we were. It was just playing a game. It was going to pull as much fear from us as possible. Creatures like this bathed in our fear, wallowing in it like little children under the streams of a sprinkler.

I tried to steel myself. I braced my shoulders and concentrated on my spell. It might have been simple, but that didn't mean it wouldn't work. I concentrated so hard my muscles tightened and my jaw clenched.

We heard the doorknob of the big closet door jiggle. It was yanked open, some of the doorframe cracking in the process. I wanted to scream. I wanted to cry a little, but I couldn't. Not now. Not with Blake's life in my hands.

"Coenum lutum!"

My eyes widened.

"Did you hear that?" I barely whispered to Blake.

"Yes," he replied, holding me tighter.

It was a female voice.

For a second, a horrible thought came to mind. If it was Tom's mother and this was her idea of getting me out of the picture, oh, what I wasn't going to say to her before she left town.

I shook my head.

It couldn't be her. She had no idea about this house, and Niles was killed before she even arrived in town. There was no way she'd be involved with this. No matter how much I didn't care for her, I didn't really believe she wanted me dead.

"Coenum lutum!"

The sound of the monster's heavy footsteps moved away from the door. There were a few seconds when we heard murmuring, but I couldn't make out what was being said. To be honest, I couldn't be sure I was hearing the murmurs from the other side of the door or if they were inside my head.

Like the voices we'd all heard when Aunt Astrid, Bea, and I ran away from this place. They were inside and outside our heads. It was like trying to locate a mouse scurrying inside a wall.

Then everything got quiet. Too quiet.

22

GALILEO

"What should we do?" I whispered.

"I think we should stay put for a little while," Blake replied. "I'm just not ready to step outside this little circle you made."

He snapped on the flashlight. I barely realized he had his arms around me. But I did realize that my foot had fallen asleep and was now rippling with pins and needles.

"So what exactly did we just witness?" Blake started. He ran through a couple possibilities, including that perhaps we'd been drugged. There was a strange mist that could have contained a hallucinogen.

"Would we see the same thing?" I asked.

"The whole thing could have been staged. This

could be some kind of elaborate hoax that was dreamed up by..." He shrugged.

"To what end? What would be the point of scaring us, and why go through the extremes of killing Niles and Patrick? That doesn't make sense."

He sat quietly for a moment. I could almost see the wheels turning in his head. I was afraid he was going to crack up. This wasn't his area of expertise. I didn't think Blake Samberg dealt with the spiritual or supernatural in his life. Everything was cut-and-dried, black or white. Any gray area was there because the problem just hadn't been solved yet. The unexplained was dangerous to a mind like his.

"What do you think it is?"

I stood up as best I could, still slightly hunched by the slanted roof.

"I think that Niles tried to conduct an experiment that went terribly wrong. He was killed by his own creation. Patrick had a hand in it, and so the creature took care of him. Now, you and I have seen it, and well, we're next if we don't stop it."

"Do you have any idea how that sounds?" Blake's words were not cruel. They were simply stated as if he were telling me the weather.

"Yes. Of course I do." But then I remembered something. "Do you know that when Galileo said the earth revolved around the sun, the authorities told him all he had to do was prove it and they'd believe?"

Blake stared at me.

"He couldn't prove it. He didn't have the technology. It took another guy, much later—I can't remember his name—to prove the earth revolved around the sun. Galileo was right. But he couldn't find a way to prove what he knew in his heart. I'm not Galileo. But I know I'm right. I just can't prove it. No matter how crazy it sounds."

I stretched my legs, thankful the pins and needles were almost gone.

Blake didn't immediately say anything. I didn't mind. That was quite a big lump of steak to digest. I let him chew on it.

It was just blind luck I happened to see something at the corner of the small room. A glint off Blake's flashlight caught my eye.

"What is that?" I pointed.

He shined the flashlight. Stuck between one of the wooden beams and the insulation was something wavy. I went to get it, when Blake's hand clamped on my arm.

"The circle." He pointed down.

He was right. There was a chance that if I stepped

out of it, I might weaken my already thin line of defense. Still, we needed to see what that was sticking out from its hiding place.

"I don't hear anything. Do you?"

Blake shook his head.

"I'll just take one step and see what happens."

"Cath."

"It'll be all right."

Carefully, I stepped one foot out of the circle. So far, so good. I stretched my torso as far as I could and reached my arm out just before lifting my other foot out of the circle.

Bang! Bang! Bang!

The little door with the crystal knob began to shake as something on the other side tried to get it open. I stepped back in the circle and focused all my effort in order to get the invisible barrier back in place.

The banging stopped, and again it was silent.

"I guess that thing knows we're in here." I wiped my brow. "Sorry about that. I guess I got a little too comfortable."

"What do we do now?" Blake whispered. "Is that thing just going to wait us out? Starve us to death?"

I had no answer. Aunt Astrid seemed pretty sure

that daylight sent that thing back to Hades. I just hoped she was right.

"Let's just wait until morning. It's all we can do." I sat back down, facing Blake. "I'm sorry I didn't make the circle bigger. We're a little cramped."

"None of this is an ideal situation." He smirked. "But I've been in worse."

"I find that hard to believe."

He went on to tell me about being stuck in a section of sewer. That wasn't as bad as when a body was found in a landfill. He had to investigate the surrounding area for clues. His favorite was when he was trapped in an elevator for over seventeen hours with a perp in handcuffs and a claustrophobic defense attorney.

"That sounds horrible." I yawned.

"It was. Especially when I was starting to like the perp more than the attorney."

I laughed and rubbed my eyes. "I can't believe I'm feeling tired. You'd think my nerves would be so strung out I'd be fidgeting and fretting with wide eyes and a clenched jaw." I showed my teeth like a shark.

"What happens if you fall asleep?" Blake asked. "Will your defense hold?"

"In theory, as long as we stay in the circle, we should be okay." I swallowed.

"What might be a good idea is for us to take turns getting a little rest. You can lean against me. I'll wake you up in twenty minutes. Then you can keep watch for me. Twenty minutes. No more."

"Okay. Why twenty?"

"Science has proven people benefit more from short naps of no more than twenty minutes than they do sleeping a couple of hours. Especially when they are under duress."

"You've got a weird factoid for just about everything, don't you?"

"Weird? I'm not the one waving silver and drawing circles to sit in."

I stuck my tongue out at him and scooted a little closer.

"Is this okay?" I rested my head on his shoulder.

"Fine," he said.

It took a matter of seconds for me to fall asleep. I didn't know how long Blake managed to stay awake before he slumped over and involuntarily stretched his leg out past the edge of the circle.

In my dream, I heard the doorknob turn. The click of the mechanism pulling back and the squeak of the old hinges were not the familiar noises I'd hear in my home. But I wasn't in my home. My eyes opened. For a second, I didn't move. The light of the flashlight had dimmed as the battery was starting to lose its strength.

When I looked up, my heart lodged in my throat.

The little door was open.

The mud creature was on its belly, reaching for Blake's foot that had involuntarily stretched out past my pitiful protection ring. It looked at me with those burning red eyes and sadistically grinned as it clamped its muddy, oozy hand around Blake's ankle.

"Blake!" I screamed.

His eyes popped open, and he instinctively reached for his gun.

The thing laughed as it proceeded to yank him closer to the door. Once it got him out there, I wouldn't be able to help.

I grabbed his free arm and tried to pull him back, but I just wasn't strong enough.

"Cath!" he yelled.

He pointed the gun at the creature and pulled the trigger. The bullet hit but was swallowed up by the mud. It barely fazed the thing. Again, Blake fired another round and another, but it didn't stop the creature. It kept pulling him.

Call it a witch's intuition if you want, but I

turned to the strange thing that we had seen sticking out from the wall. I darted across the small room in three steps and took hold of the part that was protruding from the fiberglass. With one hard yank, I pulled out a dagger with a squiggly blade.

Without taking a second to study the weapon, I charged the mud man and stabbed the forearm of the hand holding Blake's ankle.

It screamed in pain.

The blade sank through the mud and wedged itself into the floor. I backed up as Blake scurried backward like a crab out of the thing's reach.

With a grotesque tearing sound, the creature made no attempt to pull the blade from its arm. Instead, it pulled its arm back as the knife separated the muddy flesh. Like a worm being attacked by ants, the thing writhed in pain, pulled itself back from the tiny door, and disappeared into the darkness of the other room.

Carefully, I stepped forward and peeked out, not daring to step out of the circle again. I could see the windows at the far end of the room. The sky was getting lighter. Soon the sun would be up. Already I could hear birds chirping.

"Blake?" I quickly knelt next to him. "Are you all right?"

"My ankle really hurts."

I nodded. Of course it hurt. Heaven knew what kind of poison or toxins that thing was made of. Blake was probably going to need a series of tetanus shots just to be on the safe side.

He pulled himself up. Visibly trembling, he pulled himself back into the small circle.

"Well, there is a weapon. I'm afraid it has my fingerprints on it now. But maybe it will help you," I replied.

"It can't hurt."

We waited a little longer until the light outside the window was a cheerful lemony yellow.

"It looks like it's going to be a beautiful day," I joked.

"Yes, it does."

Blake looked at me. I could see in his eyes that he was struggling to understand what he'd seen. There were very few people who would be able to process something like that and remain calm. Blake seemed to be doing pretty well. I wished Bea were here. She'd be able to help him understand and ease some of the confusion and hurt that had to be swirling around inside him right now.

"I think we'd better get to my aunt's house." I took his hand as if we'd been helping each other off the floor all our lives. "She's got to be worried sick."

"I'd like that. I'd like to see your aunt."

With our eyes darting in all directions, we saw no sign of the mud monster. But we didn't want to tempt fate. Even though we had the strange knife that saved Blake's life, we both wanted out of that house. Even as he was limping, Blake took my hand, and we bolted out the front door. He couldn't run, but that didn't stop us from moving as fast as we could back to the car. It felt as if it were miles away.

Finally, once we were safely inside and zooming down the deserted morning streets to my aunt's house, Blake spoke again.

"I don't know what happened last night."

Those were the words I was afraid of hearing. Blake was in denial. He might be for the rest of his life. If only he knew that, in addition to creepy, slimy monsters, there was a myriad of beautiful things people like me could pull into focus, then he wouldn't be so scared. This world was full of mysteries, and not all of them had red eyes and sharp teeth. Some of them were as simple as loving who we love with no reason or explanation.

"But I'm glad you were there," he finished. I didn't expect that at all.

"Well, you were pretty good company too."

"You saved my life. And I don't think this was the first time."

Nor did I expect him to say those words. His expression didn't tell me anything about how he was feeling, if he were mad or scared or curious or what. All I knew was that he'd said something very nice. It was what I'd been waiting for.

I smiled until I remembered someone else had been waiting too.

I was supposed to meet Tom last night.

❧ 23 ❧

PENTAGRAM

"I'm sorry, Tom," I pleaded on the phone in Aunt Astrid's bedroom. "I couldn't get away. Really."

"Bea said you were with Detective Samberg."

"I was." Leave it to Bea to never tell a lie. Not even a little white one to save her favorite cousin's hide. "But it isn't what you think."

"You are gone for the whole night with another man who I can tell has feelings for you."

"What? We're friends, sure. He is Jake's partner. It's hard not to get to know the man when he's around all the time."

"I'm sure he made every effort to get you back in time to meet me."

There was no use arguing. Tom was mad, and I

didn't blame him. Getting stood up never felt good. What I was going to do to fix this, I wasn't sure. Part of me wasn't sure I even wanted to fix this. Everything that had to do with Tom seemed to be weighing more and more and getting bigger and bigger.

"Can you meet me this morning, Cath? Can you spare me a few minutes?"

"I'm at Aunt Astrid's. She needs me."

"Yeah. Blake is there too."

"How do you know?"

"When you didn't show up last night, I went by your house. Bea was pulling in her driveway and told me you had left with Blake. So I waited around."

"Until this morning?" I gasped. "You stalked my house?"

"No, Cath. I was worried." Tom sighed. "You've been so different since you met my mother. I just wanted to clear the air about that."

"Maybe I'm different since I met your mom because your mom doesn't think I'm good enough. She basically came right out and told me. Ask Aunt Astrid if you don't believe me. Your brother and sister married some real top-drawer individuals. You, unfortunately, won't be received by any of the proper families in Wonder Falls if you are associating with the likes of me." I did in my best Scarlett O'Hara and thought it sounded just perfect.

"That isn't what she told me. She said she thought you were fine."

"What?"

"Yeah. That's what I wanted to talk to you about. She said she thought you were very pleasant and hoped that you wouldn't judge her quiet nature with disapproval. It's obvious that you have."

That conniving woman set me up.

"She came into the café and had more than that to say to me," I replied.

"Cath, I know your gift sets you apart from everyone, but it doesn't make you better than anyone."

"I never said it did."

"I don't think you listened to my mom. I think you had made up your mind long before you met her. I know she's not the doting kind of woman like Aunt Astrid and she won't jump at your every request, but she's my mother."

"Tom, I don't think this is the right time to talk about this. And I don't think doing it over the phone is right, either."

"Well, I tried to meet with you, but you had other plans."

"I've got a family emergency right now, Tom. I'll call you when things have calmed down."

My eyes started to burn as tears of anger flooded them. I didn't wait for a good-bye when I hung up the phone. I sat on the bed with the phone in my hand and took a deep breath.

"Cath?" Bea peeked in. I was sure she'd picked up on the turmoil my soul was feeling. "Are you okay?"

I nodded and sniffled.

"I hope I didn't get you in trouble telling Tom you were with Blake."

"It's okay. If he doesn't trust me, that's on him, right?"

She sat down next to me.

"He said his mother thought I was fine," I repeated what Tom had explained to me. "Does that sound like a set-up to you, or am I being paranoid?"

"Did you tell Tom what Aunt Astrid had said?"

"No. I didn't want to get her in trouble. Plus, it is Tom's mom. What would I say?" I wiped my eyes. "Why am I so confused, Bea? Why did I turn over my own applecart?"

"You don't know?"

"No. I have no idea." I chuckled bitterly.

Bea looked at me while she took my hands in hers.

"The truth will reveal itself to you, Cath. You just have to be willing to see it."

"Okay, Bea. Thanks. That really cleared things up. You answered all my questions, and I am almost positive I can see every answer to every question *ever*." I rolled my eyes.

Bea laughed a little and squeezed my hands.

"I hate to do this to you. But you've got to clear your mind. We need your help. That sword thingy you brought home? It's got some seriously bad mojo attached to it."

"Did your mom find anything like it in her books?"

"Yup. She actually knew exactly what it was without a book, but she showed me the picture in her reference book. Of course, it has to do with *The Sequence of Ursaken*."

"Man, I hope I never hear about this sequence ever again."

Bea and I went back to the kitchen, where there were several big books open and spread out across the kitchen table.

"How's your ankle?" I asked Blake. He was sitting on the corner of Aunt Astrid's soft, comfy couch. His right foot was bare, and his pant leg was pulled up around his calf.

"Your aunt says it's going to bruise." He smirked.

I sat down on the edge of the couch next to him.

"I don't think you'll be able to get worker's comp for it," I joked.

Blake didn't smile or even smirk.

"Are you going to go home?" I asked.

"Jake and I have strict orders. We're to take this dagger to the police station and then hightail it back here before sundown."

"That sounds cryptic."

"I thought so too."

"Well, I guess I'll see you tonight."

He looked me straight in the eyes. I couldn't read his emotion at all. I guessed that was what made him a good cop, a good interrogator when he needed to be. A poker face like that could win a million dollars.

"Yes, I'll see you tonight." He reached up and tucked a strand of hair behind my ear. I couldn't help it. I grinned. There was nothing I could do to stop myself. That was when I saw the slightest change in his eyes. They softened. There might have been a wrinkle around the edges to indicate the closest I'd ever get to a smile.

It would be silly of me to say that I was twitter-pated. Cupid hadn't mowed me down with a barrage of little heart-shaped arrows. But there was something there. Blake and I were friends. Even though so many of our conversations resulted in eye rolls and sighs of frustration, he was my friend. But would he be able to accept my family and me and the cats—my goodness, the cats?

The boys left after getting whispered instructions from Aunt Astrid. Bea and I stayed in the kitchen with the cats perched on the counter like soldiers awaiting orders. When my aunt returned, she looked at me.

"I didn't want to go, Aunt Astrid. I told him, but he pulled me with him." I gulped. "I suppose I could have run away once the car stopped, but he was going in Niles's house with or without me."

"If you hadn't been there, Jake would probably be identifying Blake's body right now with the same wounds and the same gut full of mud like the others."

I shivered at the thought of Blake being alone against that creature.

"But we've got to prepare ourselves. This isn't an entity that fools around." My aunt was serious. "Now, tell me everything about last night and what you did."

It took forever to give Aunt Astrid the blow-by-blow description of what happened last night. She and Bea interrupted with questions and wanted details. I felt as if I'd done something wrong. My family acted as though they were trying to fix something I'd broken. I had to repeat myself over and over, and I had to describe the circle I made and guess how long that thing had Blake by the ankle.

Treacle could hear my thoughts and came up to nestle alongside me.

"You know they need to know everything," he purred.

"Why does it feel like they are mad at me?"

"It's just serious work, Cath. That's all."

I took a deep breath and continued.

"Is there anything to eat?" I asked quietly as I rubbed my stomach.

"We can't eat," Bea replied as she went to one of the books open on the coffee table across from where Blake had been sitting.

I looked at my aunt.

"We have to fast before we go into battle."

"Why?"

"Because we are dealing with a golem. In addition to sending it back to whence it came..." My aunt tied her hair back loosely. "We need to be prepared for it to use everything against us in order to stay here and finish what it's been summoned to do."

"Who would summon that thing? Why did

Niles want it? It's like buying a big dog and being happy it comes down with rabies. Who thinks like that?"

"I'm not so sure it was Niles."

"What?" I gasped.

"While you were gone last night, we saw a car skulking around," my aunt said.

"Oh, that was Tom. He said he parked outside and waited for me to come home. Creepy. I know. I've made such a mess of things with him that…"

"No. We knew Tom was out there," Bea interrupted.

"I don't know how to feel about that. I think I'll go with… humiliated. Yup, I'm humiliated you guys knew Tom was stalking around my house." I shook my head and stroked Treacle in an attempt to soothe myself.

"Tom can't help the way he feels about you any more than I can." Treacle head-butted me.

"That still doesn't make it right," I replied and went on to listen to my aunt.

"No. There was a woman out there too," Aunt Astrid said. "I tried to get a look at her face, but it was too dark. So I decided to try the old-fashioned way. Walking up and talking to her."

"What?" I looked at Bea. "Doesn't your mother

know it is dangerous to approach strangers in a car? What if they kidnapped you?"

Finally, my aunt smirked a little as she shook her head.

"Mom said the woman had the sloppiest, most ramshackle protection spell surrounding her. It was like she threw it together from a bunch of different spells and only got part of it right in each one," Bea added.

"I could peek through the holes in it, but I didn't get a good look at her," Aunt Astrid continued.

I thought as hard as I could but couldn't imagine anyone who might have had anything to do with Niles that they'd want him dead. The women who sought his services adored him. And without the appointment book that melted into mud, there was no way without going door-to-door that we could find out who Aunt Astrid might have seen.

"How do you know she was watching my house?" I asked.

"She used binoculars. And then she drove by slowly a couple dozen times before parking in front of my house to stare at yours."

"Did you get a license plate number? Make and model of the car? Anything?"

"The car had those dark reflectors covering the

plates. It was a Lexus and blue or black. Some dark color. I told Jake, but he said that unless she did something to vandalize the house or trespass or something, we were out of luck." Bea stroked Peanut Butter.

I let out a big sigh.

"So what do we do now?" I looked at my watch. The entire morning had already passed. My stomach was growling. I was getting a headache, and we still had several hours before nightfall.

"I'm glad you asked. I've got a list," my aunt replied. And it was a long list that included not only generating the most industrial-strength protection spell ever but also cloaking our psyches so the thing couldn't see our thoughts. We had to have a parallel sight. That was to ensure we'd be able to see any help this golem might have lurking in the shadows. Finally, and probably the worst thing of all, we had to implement *sonitus perimo*.

"How are we going to fight this thing if we can't hear anything?" I asked. *Sonitus perimo* was the temporary blocking of the sound. We would all technically be deaf for an indefinite amount of time. It would last the duration of the conflict, but for obvious reasons, it was very dangerous.

"We will each face a corner of the pentagram. The

correct pentagram." Aunt Astrid chuckled and shook her head as she remembered the childish rendition that was painted in Niles's backyard. "If we prepare correctly, there will be no reason for us to worry about our hearing."

"But what if something sneaks up behind us?" I asked. "That's what I'd do if I were the bad guy."

"That's why we will have our backs to each other in a tight circle. As long as we stay focused on the task at hand." My aunt smiled.

"You make it sound like we're not doing anything more than a regular housecleaning spell," Bea said.

"That's how I want you to look at it. This is just another spell that will rid Niles's house of some dirt. Mud. Mud in the shape of a man, to be exact. Now…" Aunt Astrid looked at her watch. "We have a lot to do and little time to do it."

"Do we really have to wait until nighttime?" I asked. "We can't make a sweep of the house during the bright daytime hours?"

My aunt just shook her head.

"What about the boys?" Bea asked. "What are they going to do when they get home? How are we going to keep them safe while we're at Niles's house?"

"Once they are here, I've got a sleep spell ready

for them. They'll rest and wake up when the whole thing is over." My aunt was talking as she stuffed a huge carpetbag with candles, crystals, semiprecious stones, and a few other weapons for our battle.

"Why did they take that dagger?" I grumbled. "It stopped that creature last night. We could have used that."

"I could just see you running at that thing like Mel Gibson in *Braveheart*," Bea said. "All wild-eyed and hysterical."

"I think I'd be more like PeeWee Herman," I replied, making Bea and my aunt laugh.

"All right, girls. Time's up. We'd better get started."

❦ 24 ❦

DEAD BOLT

It might sound strange, but the lower the sun sank in the sky, the more energy I had. We had been preparing all day long. Even the cats all looked shinier and fuller, as the endurance and protection spells were for them as much as us. Marshmallow and Treacle were able to sit and breathe quite calmly as they channeled their energy. Peanut Butter, just graduating from the kitten stage to the young cat stage, was busy hunting his tail.

Bea radiated from the inside out, and Aunt Astrid looked ten years younger. I didn't bother to look at myself. With my luck, all this extra magic probably affected me like a second puberty, complete with acne and mood swings.

The sun went down around eight o'clock this

time of year. The shadows had stretched their fingers across the grass. Porch lights were popping on along the street. And along with the nighttime sky came a thick blanket of clouds. Lightning flashed across the sky, and a low rumble shook the ground.

"Did you guys know if was going to rain tonight?" I asked.

"That's good. That will hide us from any snoopy neighbors who might look out their windows or think to keep an eye on Niles's house," Aunt Astrid said. "We'd better get going."

Just as my aunt hoisted her bag over her shoulder and Bea and I grabbed the books we needed, the rain started. It was a downpour.

"I'll get a couple umbrellas," I said and darted to the closet where my aunt kept them. Just as I was about to ask who wanted the one with the sunflowers, I froze.

There was a tremendous crack of thunder. Below it was that horrible, hateful scream of the golem. Or as I had come to call it, the mud monster.

That same horrible scream that we'd heard that first night at Niles's house shook the pictures on the walls. It was the same sound Blake and I had heard last night as the muddy golem pulled itself from the putrid pond and when I stabbed it with the curvy blade.

I stared at Bea. "It's here. How can it be here?"

"*It travels in the ground. It was following us when we were on the property that night.*" Marshmallow said to me.

"How does it know where we are?" I asked.

"How does evil always know where good is?" my aunt answered cryptically. "The only thing that has changed, girls, is location. We won't be seeking it out. It has already made its presence known."

"Yeah, and it's in our backyard," I muttered then looked at Bea, who looked as if she'd just swallowed a fly. "What's the matter?"

"Jake and Blake will be coming back here. They are probably on their way right now."

Terror gripped my heart. The boys would be walking into an ambush.

"No time to waste!" Aunt Astrid yelled. "Bea, try calling the station and tell Jake not to come home."

Bea darted for the phone.

"Cath, tell the cats to position themselves as we discussed. You help me get the candles and stones ready. Grab some sage. It can't hurt."

I did as I was told. But just as I put my hand on a

bundle of sage, just as I heard Bea ask for Jake or Detective Samberg, the lights went out.

"Hello? Hello?" Bea yelled into the phone. "It's dead!"

My aunt struck a match, calmly lit a white candle, then held it up to her face. It was the only thing illuminated in the whole room. I was never scared of my aunt. Never. But I thought at that moment that if I were the mud monster and I saw my aunt's glowing face, I might reconsider my whole idea of killing.

"Calm down, girls. The storm is outside."

I grabbed the matches that were always on Aunt Astrid's coffee table and lit the bundle of sage. Reciting the cleansing chant I'd been saying since I was a little girl, I walked through the living room, paying special attention to the front and back doors and the windows. It took no time to work through the kitchen and the downstairs rooms. I headed upstairs.

Just as I was finishing my ritual, I looked outside. I tried not to. I really did. But like driving past a car accident, you couldn't help but feel you had to look... you must look, if for no other reason than to see it wasn't as bad as you thought. The rain pummeled the ground just past the back patio.

There, illuminated by a flash of lightning, was the mud monster. It stared up at me.

"As long as you're looking at me, you aren't getting inside. Aunt Astrid and Bea can finish getting ready. And you can get ready to go back to where you came from." I waved the sage across the window, never taking my eyes off the thing.

Bang! Bang! Bang!

I nearly jumped out of my skin then turned when I heard the knock on the front door. My heart sank as soon as I turned back to the window and the lightning showed me the thing was gone.

"Don't open it!" I screamed. "Don't do it!"

Bea looked at me as I teetered, tripped, and staggered down the steps as if I were drunk, only after she was holding the door open.

"Tom?"

"So you don't want them to let me in?"

I grabbed his hand and yanked him in the house, and Bea slammed the door shut behind him and snapped the dead bolt back in place.

"No, Tom." I nearly started to cry. "What are you doing here?"

"I needed to talk to you."

"Oh… for Pete's sake, Tom!" I shuddered. "Now is not the time."

"What's going on here?" he asked.

Suddenly, the thing outside bellowed with anger that it had missed its chance to either get another victim or get inside the house.

"You need to sit down and be quiet," I said, my eyes burning as I pushed the tears back.

"Cath, you can't talk to me like that." He was trying to be touchy-feely when we were in a life-or-death situation.

"What? Someone needs to! I didn't invite you over!"

"Cath, you are really being selfish. I'm trying to tell you that our relationship is in trouble, and you want to run around playing scary movie in order to avoid facing me."

"Tom, can I make you some tea?" Bea interrupted.

"Yes." Tom smirked. "Yes, thank you, Bea."

"Bea, do we really have time for tea?" I wiped my eyes in frustration.

"It'll just take a moment," she replied coldly.

Aunt Astrid watched the entire thing unfold but said nothing. At least she didn't say anything out loud, even though her lips were moving. I wasn't even sure if she saw Tom. In the heightened state of being we were all in, I had no idea what my aunt could see or what Bea could see. All I knew was that I was ready to attack a demon, and Tom was zapping all my energy because he wanted to argue about our relationship. Who was selfish?

"Cath, would you go get Mom's sweater that's hanging on the chair in her office? She's going to need it," Bea said gently.

I sighed before stomping off down the hallway to Aunt Astrid's office. I felt like a child and was mad at Bea for sending me out of the room as though I were one. When I came back, Tom was slumped over the counter. Bea was taking his teacup and putting it gently in the sink.

"Did you kill him?" I asked.

"No man is going to talk to my cousin that way," Bea snapped. "No. I didn't kill him. But I can't say I didn't think about it for a second. He gets in the house and is safe and sound due to our efforts, and Jake could come face-to-face with—"

"Don't, Bea. Jake and Blake will be safe. They will be."

The thunder clapped as the rain pounded down. Aunt Astrid pushed two of her armchairs to the far walls. The candles were placed in a triangular pattern on the floor with the crystals in a complementary pattern. There was a bowl in the center, and the cats were unusually quiet, staying close to my aunt as she mumbled incessantly.

"Treacle, are you doing okay?"

"It's getting close, Cath. We need to hurry."

"Bea, are you ready?" I tried to hurry her along.

Bea grabbed a clear glass bowl and filled it with water.

"Yes. I'm ready."

We went to my aunt and took our positions around the candles and stones. The cats were there with us. Before I even had a chance to get focused, my aunt walked to the front door.

"Wait." I stared. "What are you doing?"

Aunt Astrid began to recite the elaborate words that only Bea and I could decipher. She led the chant. We were to reply in unison. But I didn't realize what she was going to do.

"Aunt Astrid, don't!"

"Mom?"

Aunt Astrid faced her heavy door, reciting the words. Without hesitating she snapped the dead bolt back and took hold of the knob.

"Mom!"

25

BOTCHED

"Bea! Do as you're told!" Aunt Astrid scolded as she pulled the door wide open.

There it was. The mud monster stood right at the door, towering over my aunt. It grinned as it stared down at her. But she stood straight, toe to toe with that thing. The words poured from her mouth. Bea and I remained where we were. We were both on autopilot, paralyzed by fear as we mumbled our parts of the chants. My entire body trembled. Bea was crying. Aunt Astrid had never looked more threatening as she confronted this demon that had been summoned by accident by a no-talent wannabe.

The thing began to fidget and writhe as we recited our words.

"No!" Aunt Astrid ordered.

The mud monster was speaking to her. There was a low hum in the back of my head that was like an echo traveling down a tunnel. Then I heard it. A voice I had heard before.

"Kill her! You must do as I say!" It was screaming. The female voice was screaming for the thing to kill Aunt Astrid! Suddenly, I remembered where I'd heard it before. My heart pounded as it had when I was running with Bea. I looked straight ahead of me as the dimensions waved as if I were looking through a fish tank.

"Dolores Eversol! You did this!"

The creature screamed as lightning flashed madly.

It wasn't Niles. Niles didn't botch up *The Sequence of Ursaken*! Dolores Eversol did it! She summoned the demon!

And right now she was at Niles's house, with those crystal balls that were in the garden on the altar we had discovered. The rain was pouring down in sheets. Flashes of lightning revealed the creature writhing even more as it struggled to find a way over the threshold in order to do its master's bidding.

Bea was awash in sweat. Her body trembled as she recited the words that would help keep this thing on the edge without crossing.

It was beginning to feel as if the thing's energy was depleting. Aunt Astrid, Bea, and I continued the chant. The rain pounded. Thunder shook the whole house. Still, the thing stayed where it was, screaming in frustration and rage.

"You will return to where you've come from, you foul beast!" Aunt Astrid screamed.

Before I knew what she was doing, she lifted an ax, swung with all her might, and took the head clear off the creature. It slapped against the wall then slid to the floor with a sickening thud.

The body remained standing for several seconds before it fell with a loud, wet thump. The rain continued to pour down, washing the thing away as it would any pile of dirt.

Aunt Astrid pulled a scarf from around her shoulders then scooped up the grotesque head. The eyes still blinked and rolled madly. Its mouth continued to form its hateful words and screams, but nothing but a gurgling, drowning sound could be heard from it.

I reached down to scoop up the crystals Aunt Astrid had placed in our circle. They had changed from perfect shards of white and pink crystal to sickly-looking black opaque stones.

Quickly I transferred them over to my aunt.

Without flinching she shoved the black rocks into the open maw of the mud monster. The sounds it made were enough to make my stomach crinkle in disgust.

"Open the back door," she instructed. I ran ahead of her, snapped the lock, and slid the sliding back door wide open.

"Now, you will go back to the worms and the dirt and the darkness!" Aunt Astrid yelled at the head still clinging to its earthly form.

Its eyes still stared at us with so much hatred as Bea took the gardening shovel and began to dig a hole. I used my hands to help clear away the mud. Aunt Astrid placed the thing in the ground face-down. We covered it up with the mud we'd dug up and listened.

"Are we done?" I asked. I looked up into the rain and let the downpour wash as much of the dirt off as I could. "Can we please have something to eat now?"

"Yes. It's done." Aunt Astrid walked into the house. Bea and I followed. It took several seconds for us to realize there was a person standing in the open front door.

"I hate you!" Dolores Eversol screamed. She literally screamed at us like a spoiled teenager responding to a parent who wouldn't buy her a car. "Do you have any idea what you've done?"

Had she not had a gun in one hand and a knife in the other, I would have had some seriously sarcastic things to say to her. But as it was, I kept my mouth shut.

"I was sure the police were going to take care of you. You had more of a motive to kill Niles than me," Dolores babbled.

"I had no reason to kill Niles. Who are you, and what are you talking about?"

We all had our hands up. I felt like a dope and looked at the cats, who were still in their trance. It might take a few minutes, or it might take an hour for them to completely snap out of it. I looked around for something to throw at Dolores, but nothing was within reach.

"That's Dolores Eversol," I hissed. "She's the one who botched up *The Sequence of Ursaken*." I raised my voice over the sound of the rain coming in from both open doors.

"You're the one who did this?" Bea chuckled. "I don't think you could have screwed it up any more if you had tried on purpose."

Dolores grimaced. "Oh, you think I'm funny. Just a joke compared to you three? You think I don't know what you are? What your family is? You think you are so special, seeing into the future and doing your little healing things." She waved the knife at Bea, scowling at her. "Oh no. I know all about the Greenstones. Niles always said you were the real deal. A psychic. A healer. I guess they just kept you around because they needed a good dishwasher at the café." She hissed at me.

"Are you off your meds?" I scoffed.

"Cath, I don't know if that is helpful." Aunt Astrid cleared her throat.

"What, Aunt Astrid? Did you see what she did with *The Sequence of Ursaken*?" I rolled my eyes so Dolores would continue staring at me. "I'm going to believe she can shoot straight or has the stomach to slice me up after seeing what she did with that spell? A kindergartener with a blue crayon could do a better job conjuring."

"Cath? You might want to be quiet." Bea looked nervous, but I ignored her.

"Tell me, Dolores." I took a step closer. "When you aren't out making a joke of centuries-old protection spells, are you in your house, trying to get your broom to fly? You know that is just an old wives' tale. We don't actually fly on brooms."

I was afraid that I might have guessed correctly.

The look on Dolores's face was pure rage. Without saying a word she raised her gun, took aim, and then...

Pop!

The bullet whizzed right past me, imbedding itself in the wooden frame just above the door. It would have been a direct hit had Treacle, Marshmallow, and Peanut Butter remained in their trance too much longer.

The cats jumped at Dolores with their claws extended and their mouths wide open. I loved how it took these magnificent creatures mere seconds to revert to their wild heritage.

They scratched and clawed, hissing and screeching as they attacked our assailant, knocking her off balance. She crashed to the hard wooden floor, giving Bea and me just enough time to kick the gun away and pin her down. She screamed and cried and fought like a woman possessed. I thought she was.

"My gift?" I said to her confused and angry face. "I can talk to animals."

I will admit that the look on her face was priceless. She didn't see that coming, and as I kneeled on her right arm and Bea kneeled on her left, Aunt Astrid stepped up to bind her until we could get the police here.

"I bind you, Dolores Eversol, from doing harm to anyone or especially harm to yourself."

"You can't bind me. I'm the greatest psychic since Rasputin. I've got greater powers than Merlin. You'll pay for this. I'll make sure you and your whole family suffer. You'll remember my name every day when you wake each morning with agony and fear. In your future, I see…"

"I bind your tongue, that you may not speak ill of anyone. I bind your power, that you may be helpless. I bind you now, from feet to brow," I said as I leaned on her arm. Treacle came and sat on her chest, staring down at her face.

She looked up at my big black cat and finally stopped. She tried to open her mouth, but nothing came but a silent scream.

"What are you doing?"

All of us, including Treacle, turned to look. Tom had regained consciousness.

"Um…" was all I could say. So much for thinking under pressure.

"This woman is sick, Tom. But the power is out because of the storm. We can't call for an ambulance or the police. We have to keep her here."

"Well, get off her," Tom insisted.

"She had a gun." I pointed to the pistol that was just out of reach in the foyer. "She took a shot at us. The bullet is in the wall." I pointed to the back door, which was still open, the sheer curtains flapping wildly in the wind as though we were in some gothic horror story.

The candles that were in our circle managed to stay lit, but one good gust of wind, and we'd be back in complete darkness.

"How could I have slept through this?" Tom glared at me. "We were talking and…"

"Tom, I know you're confused, but you have to understand that we had a job to do. It was important and—"

My aunt tried to be nice. She did. Tom wasn't having any of it.

"With all due respect, Astrid, this is between Cath and me." He looked at me with anger behind his eyes. "You knocked me out, didn't you? You put some kind of spell on me to get me out of the way."

"Tom, this isn't really the right time for this," I pleaded.

"She didn't do any such thing."

Bea stood up. Dolores wasn't going anywhere. She was bound up tighter than a Regency romance corset.

"I did it. You were not speaking to Cath the way a man should speak to the woman he cares about. We needed her help, and we needed her focused. If I let you keep on the way you were going, the way you are going now, it could have gotten her killed."

"So you've got your whole family in our business?"

"That's what family is for, Tom. You know what I am. You said it was okay. That you accepted it." I didn't want to cry, but I felt the tears rushing over my eyeballs. This was embarrassing. "Sometimes that calls for me to make some harsh decisions. Snap judgments. I'm not perfect."

"Yeah, I know what you are." Tom sighed. He reached behind him and pulled out his handcuffs, which he always wore in addition to his gun. He walked over to Dolores, rolled her on her back, and slipped the cuffs on her. She didn't resist. She couldn't.

With her up and out of the way, we were able to close the doors and light a few more candles. After about ten more minutes, the lights came back on. Bea dialed Jake, who had been stuck with Blake in the lab at the station when the power went out.

"Are you all right?" Jake asked.

"We're fine. But if you guys could get over here

and get this lunatic out of my mom's house, that would be good."

"We'll be right there."

"Jake and Blake are on their way," Bea announced as she started to pull some things out of the fridge to make us all something to eat.

"I'd like meat." I pointed to all the salad fixings Bea had in her arms. "Bacon. Maybe salami. Something with substance."

Aunt Astrid was tired and sat next to Dolores. It was kind of creepy, seeing such opposites so close to each other. From the look of it, Dolores had gone off the deep end. Her eyes watched something that none of us could see. She fidgeted as if she was hoping there was a chink in the binding spell. Not if I put it on her. I wasn't as good a witch as Aunt Astrid, but there were a few things I knew I could do. Keeping this woman bound was one of them.

"Do you want something to eat?" I looked at Tom, who was rubbing his head.

"I could eat," he replied but didn't smile.

Bea walked up to him and put her hand on his arm.

"I'm sorry for what I did to you, Tom."

"I don't know what you expect me to say, Bea.

This isn't normal." He shook his head as he looked at my cousin. This was not good.

The strange thing was that I was starting to know exactly how Dolores was feeling. I wanted to speak. There were a thousand things I wanted to say, and not a single word would form in my mouth.

Seeing Bea's reaction made me sad. If Tom didn't want anyone to mess with him, he shouldn't have gotten so out of control. This was no different from his mother making it clear that I wasn't good enough for him.

"She didn't drug you, though," Treacle whispered.

"What do I do? I don't think sorry is good enough. I don't even know if I am sorry. What's wrong with me?"

"You have to do what your heart says, Cath. There is no other way."

Treacle rubbed against my leg then trotted off to join the other cats, who were all getting treats for a job well done.

"Are you going to tell me what I missed?" He looked at me with very little expression on his face.

I shook my head.

"Figures." He twisted his jaw and looked up to where the bullet hole was in Aunt Astrid's back door frame. "I'm going to make this easy for you, Cath.

This isn't working. I think we need some time apart."

He pushed himself away from the counter and headed toward the front door.

"Tom, wait. Don't you want to talk about this?"

"Yeah. I did," he snapped. "But you had a million other things and other people you were more interested in talking to. It's too late for that now, Cath. You're too late. My mother is leaving to visit my sister tomorrow. I've got to say goodbye to her." He looked down for a moment as if he were waiting for me to say something or stop him.

"I don't know what to say."

"Don't say anything, Cath. Just don't."

He yanked open the front door and stomped out. The rain was still coming down but not as hard as it had been. Off in the distance, I could see more lightning coming. The storm wasn't over.

The engine of his truck roared to life, and within seconds, Tom was peeling out of the driveway. There was nothing left but the smell of diesel. I closed the door and looked at my family. I couldn't help but notice Dolores seemed very pleased with the drama unfolding in front of her.

"What are you looking at, Glinda?" I barked. *The*

Wizard of Oz witch reference wasn't lost on her, and she frowned in anger. It made me feel a little better.

"I'm so sorry, Cath." Bea came rushing over. "I shouldn't have done what I did. I should have… just told Tom to leave."

I shrugged. I wanted to cry. Really, I did. But it felt as if I was beyond crying. The mourning had already taken place somewhere between the death of Niles Freudenfur and meeting Tom's mother. I'd already said goodbye and cried. Maybe they weren't literal tears, but they were no less heartfelt.

26

A RIPPLE IN THE UNIVERSE

It was amazing the difference a day could make. Aunt Astrid often said that. After Jake sent a squad car with two uniformed officers to the house to pick up the trash that was Dolores Eversol, we each retired to one of the bedrooms to get some rest.

Aunt Astrid, as usual, fell asleep with Marshmallow in her study on the chaise lounge. Bea slept in her mom's bed with Peanut Butter, who was so exhausted the kitty had to be carried like a wet sandbag. After the main event with the mud monster, Peanut Butter's tail was still on the loose, and she had spent another half hour chasing it around the legs of chairs, through the railing of the staircase, and on the rug in front of the fireplace.

Treacle and I took the upstairs bedroom. I was tired, but I wasn't as exhausted as I thought I'd be after doing battle. It was scary. But for some reason, I had no doubt we were going to pull through this one. No one got hurt. The magic hangover was almost nonexistent. It was almost as though the universe had already decided that there was no room for mud monsters and loonies like Dolores Eversol in this realm.

Not that we didn't work hard. Everything just fell into place perfectly.

But then I had a weird thought. So much of the angst I was feeling over the past couple of weeks was due to my indecision about Tom. Don't get me wrong—the idea that we had broken up made me feel a twinge in my heart that pushed tears to my eyes. I was sorry it had come to this end. Who wouldn't prefer a mutual breakup in which we could tell each other our good qualities and wish each other well with at least the thought that maybe we'd share a coffee some time in the future?

But that wasn't what had happened with Tom. Our breakup was a rip that left a jagged edge and an exposed, tender area that was painful to touch.

However, how clear was the sky now that the

breakup had become official? I wouldn't say that I didn't feel better about it. A weight had been lifted.

"*Do you think that my clinging to my relationship with Tom might have caused a ripple in the universe that contributed to Dolores making a mess of* The Sequence of Ursaken?" I asked as I stroked Treacle, who had snuggled against my side on the bed.

"*That is a very deep thought. Where did it come from?*"

I explained my thought process and waited for my cat's sage response.

"*You're overtired. Get some rest, and you'll be making sense again in no time.*"

"*I'm being serious. Now that we've broken up, my senses seem to be back in line. Like I had a visit from a celestial chiropractor. Could the universe have been telling me that it was time for me to let go? Then when I did, peace returned to the land?*" I scratched him behind the ears.

"*Either that, or you were under a spell that is now removed.*"

"What?" This was an avenue I hadn't explored.

"*Tom's mother. Aunt Astrid picked up on it. So did I. She has been using her sophomoric witching skills to manipulate the people around her for years. You don't think there was a possibility she was doing that with you and Tom?*"

I gasped.

"*I'm not saying that's it. But your family would never*

put a spell on you. I don't think Dolores had the skills, either. Not without giving herself away. Everything was all about her, you know."

I nodded.

"But the whole history of her other children marrying into wealth or privilege and Tom being sort of the black sheep in her eyes sort of makes me think she might have had a hand in it."

"My gosh, Treacle. Did I play right into her hands?"

"Maybe."

"So much for my feeling better after the Band-Aid had been ripped off."

"No. You of all people shouldn't feel that way."

"Why? Maybe I just blew off the best thing to ever come along for me."

"Just like the truth always has a way of surfacing, the universe and the Great Creator always bring things together that are meant to be. That's how it has been since the Big Bang, right?"

I took a deep breath and let it out slowly.

"If you and Tom are meant to be together, he'll find his way back to you."

"You think so?"

"Only if you are meant to be." Treacle yawned.

I didn't say any more. What was there to say to this? I couldn't go back to Tom and say, "I just wanted to give it another try in case it was your mom putting her negative mojo on us." He'd really flip over that.

Then there was the fact that it felt better to be free of him. He wasn't a burden in the traditional sense of the word, but he was not happy, and that made me unhappy. It was like leaving a faucet on. The energy just kept pouring out.

Treacle stretched his paws out on me, and I closed my eyes.

I saw my mother in my dream.

❧

USUALLY, SADLY, WHEN I DREAMED ABOUT my mother, she was reaching for me as that mysterious thing pulled her underneath my bed. Either I'd have her hands in mine and they'd slip, or she'd be just a fraction of an inch out of reach.

Before I could make a move, she'd slip away from me, screaming, her eyes wide and terrified as she was pulled into that blackness.

I had been only nine years old when they took her from me. It left a hole in my heart as dark as that space under my bed all those years ago.

But this dream was different. She was not in my

childhood bedroom. She was nowhere near the bed. Instead, she was sitting at Aunt Astrid's kitchen table. She and Aunt Astrid looked so much alike, except my aunt had blond hair that was graying. My mother, on the other hand, had dark-brown hair, and it was graying at the temples.

They were laughing about something. I couldn't tell you what. It didn't matter. All I saw was my mom laughing. I heard the sound of her voice as she chuckled over something my aunt had said. That voice had been the sound of safety and love since I was just a couple of weird cells in her tummy. I'd always know that sound even after so many years of not hearing it.

She was laughing, and I started to laugh too. When I woke up, I started to cry. I didn't want the dream to be over. Not yet. I just wanted a second to ask her what was so funny. Was it something I did or said? Did Bea do something that was funny? Were they remembering a story from their own childhood together?

I took another deep breath and wiped my eyes. Treacle purred but didn't dare move or pry his own eyes open. He was happy to remain in the bed, so I slid out and left him there.

Downstairs, Aunt Astrid was up and had coffee

brewing. She turned around from the fridge, holding some grapes in a bag.

"Did you see her?" she asked.

That was all I needed to hear. The floodgates opened, and I ran to my aunt. She folded me in her arms and held tight as I sobbed. Was this for my mom or Tom or maybe even Niles and Patrick, who had died needlessly? I didn't know. But I felt the love from my aunt as if it were my real mother holding me.

"What does it mean?" I sniffled.

"What do you think it means?"

"I want to believe it means she can see me, Aunt Astrid. I want to believe that."

"Cath, there are so many things in this world we don't know. How can we ever expect to grasp what happens on the other planes of existence? The one the mud-monster came from. The one your mom is on. One thing is for sure. When they want to get a message to us, they will find a way." She smoothed my hair back.

"You dreamed of her too?"

She nodded and gave me a kiss on the cheek.

Just then, Bea showed up.

"I had a beautiful dream," she said as she rubbed her eyes like a child just getting up.

"Really? What was it?"

"I dreamed that Jake built me a raised garden in the backyard, and it was so big I was growing pumpkins and zucchini and tomatoes the size of grapefruits out there. We were able to eat organic for an entire winter."

"That was your beautiful dream?"

"Well, yeah. It doesn't get much better than that." She shuffled over to the coffeepot. "Really, mom? You know we're trying to cut down on caffeine."

"I thought that was only when Jake was with you."

As if on cue, there was a jingle of keys in the front door. Within seconds, Jake and Blake were strolling into the kitchen, looking tired and worn out but in all other respects safe and sound.

"Two Earl Grey teas, please," Bea sang.

"I'll take the hard stuff," I mumbled, wiping my eyes and instinctively pulling my hair back as if that were somehow going to make me look presentable. "Blake, coffee?"

"You're reading my mind." He limped over to the sofa and sat down. I brought him a cup of coffee but didn't sit down. I didn't want to seem too interested. I wasn't. I'd just broken up with Tom. How would it look if I just started throwing out signals that I was interested in Blake? Again? Was I interested in him? Again? Had I ever stopped being interested in him? I was getting a headache.

"How's the ankle?"

"It feels like I was running full speed and stepped into a gopher hole."

"I'm sorry."

"Blake, I'll take a look at that in a minute. Maybe I can help," Bea said as she handed Jake a cup to hold as the hot water started to boil.

"How did things turn out last night?" Aunt Astrid asked as she placed some grapes, slices of cheese, pepperoni, and French bread in the middle of her kitchen table and invited everyone to help themselves. Except Blake, of course, whom she loaded up a plate for and presented to him as if it were an Academy Award.

"Dolores Eversol confessed, in a way. However, she holds you responsible for her actions." Jake chuckled as he looked at Aunt Astrid.

"Me?"

"See, I told you it was her who tipped off the cops that Aunt Astrid had something to do with bumping off Niles," I said with a mouth full of cheese.

"You sound like a character in a Sam Spade movie." Bea laughed.

"She claims that you were tormenting her in her sleep because she was going to take over Niles's business and be the top psychic in town if not the entire state," Jake said.

"Everyone has to have a goal." My aunt shrugged and took a bite of bread.

"She confessed to using that weapon Cath saw in Niles's house to stab Niles and Patrick. That would ensure they wouldn't come back."

"Come back?" I asked.

"From the dead," Jake replied.

"Of course. How silly of me. I should have known," I replied, nodding and tapping my finger to my temple.

"We have every reason to believe she was planning to use it on you, too, had we not confiscated it," Blake replied. "Not that it mattered since she had a Plan B."

"There is still one strange thing we can't figure out," Jake added. "How she was able to subdue both Niles and Patrick? Niles was old, so a lucky blow could have easily done it. But Patrick, he was young, healthy, and strong. It is a real mystery."

"I tried to explain to Jake that individuals under

certain strenuous circumstances, whether they be self-imposed or from an outside source, can exhibit unnatural strength," Blake said.

"Like being possessed," I added.

"Exactly. If she sincerely thought she had some kind of paranormal gift that gave her the strength to lift a car, she just might be able to lift a car."

I looked at Blake and wondered what he was thinking. He had seen the muddy golem. It had given him a nasty thing on his ankle to remember him by. He didn't seem shaken up by it, but he didn't appear to be in any hurry to discuss it, either. What was wrong with him? If it were me, I'd be repeating the story to anyone who would listen and going into graphic detail about how the thing stank, had red eyes, and looked a little like poop.

"So what's going to happen to her?" Bea asked.

"She's looking at third-degree murder. They will probably try to say she is mentally unfit for trial or use the insanity defense. They might get it. She's pretty far out there."

It didn't take long for me to shove six slices of salami in my mouth, along with several pieces of torn bread and a dozen grapes—all before I had my first sip of coffee. After my beautiful dream, some good food, and my entire family around me, I was feeling pretty good.

When I looked up, I noticed that Blake was looking right at me. I looked back at him without the usual giddiness or awkwardness or even the hatefulness I sometimes felt around him when it seemed as if he was talking down to me. I was sure I'd feel that way again. Give it twenty minutes. But as for right now, I looked back at him, knowing that he'd experienced the paranormal with me. He saw it. I saw it. We didn't need to talk it to death. Not right now. Maybe not ever. I was going to let him take the lead. That was an idea I really liked.

As the second cup of coffee was being poured, the phone rang.

Aunt Astrid answered and exchanged a few pleasantries before handing the phone to me.

"Who is it?" I asked with my back to the rest of the group as Bea fussed over Blake's ankle.

"It's Tom."

I swallowed hard, but my mouth had already gone dry.

"Hello?"

"Hi, Cath. Do you have a minute?"

"Sure," I said.

ABOUT THE AUTHOR

Harper Lin is the *USA TODAY* bestselling author of 6 cozy mystery series including *The Patisserie Mysteries* and *The Cape Bay Cafe Mysteries*.

When she's not reading or writing mysteries, she loves going to yoga classes, hiking, and hanging out with her family and friends.

www.HarperLin.com

CPSIA information can be obtained
at www.ICGtesting.com
Printed in the USA
BVHW032012220421
605655BV00015B/173